Sophie's Wildflowers

By

Sahara Sutter

DISCLAIMER

This book was written by a human wishing to share a
unique story regarding the challenges and unforeseen
connections that echo through life and across
generations.

INTRODUCTION

The old photographs portray an idyllic life within a monochrome, small, sleepy southern town. Coming of age during mounting unrest awakens reality to the contrast between social enlightenment and mayhem from the mid-1950s to 1962. Decades after her untimely death, an event detailed in Beyond the Garden – God's Houseplants, Sophie's recently discovered diary reveals an intriguing means to survival amidst the insightful writings of a wealthy girl during troubled times in DeLand, Florida.

Sophie brilliantly creates a twisted legacy that escapes and misleads all for over half a century after her untimely death and provides the inescapable connections that echo through generations.

Optimism befriends fairytales within each hope and dream as deceit walks among us, living and yet unseen.

DEDICATION

To S.R. and those

who believe in the dreams of others and

make the world better for all.

ACKNOWLEDGMENT

In gratitude to Mr. Chaffee, a High School English Teacher, and Marie Anderson, Major, USMC.

Special thanks to artist Diane Erickson.

diane1erickson@gmail.com

TABLE OF CONTENTS

BROKEN BITS OF ONCE UPON A TIME

Cindy Peterson, that's me. I am a "60-something" woman and, save a few short days, a lifetime orphan. Decades of searching my history have resulted in feeling abandoned at the doorstep of the wrong planet. However, opportunity encountered historical reality to uncover a fascinating story of my Mother, Sophie Sherman, growing up and matching wits with secrets, murder, and ample mayhem.

Not too long ago, and very nearby... **fast forward to today!**

MARGARITA MOONLIGHT

In every aspect, it was so far from my everyday reality. I am lying face-up in a hammock. The morning world is awash in crisp hues of blue as shreds of white and pink cotton candy clouds stretch toward the horizon. Upon the endless sky, a handmade kite of part palm frond, a few plastic straws precariously held together with drops of super glue, the small hole-less part of an old sheet, and a few rubber bands tied together for a tail try to fly upon fishing line among squawking seagulls. A warm breeze caresses my face and tickles my bare toes as the aptly named *Chasing Hope* sailboat gently sways to the gentle rhythm of the Caribbean Sea below and soft trade winds above.

I was mentally and physically in a place where each day flowed graciously into the next. Footprints upon pristine beaches were gently smoothed by water lapping the sand over unmeasured time. The skies blushed with pride as a jealous seagull reached to touch the fading glory as the sun melted into a grateful sea of gold and moonlight softened upon endless ripples streaming into eternity. It was paradise in every direction and saturating every sense as I became comfortable with flip-flops, ponytails, and warm beer as reality slipped below the horizon along with the banishment of the ultimate evil master – my alarm clock.

For the moment, I forgot about life. I believe in abandoning all strife. I am optimistic there is a Heaven.

Somewhere floating upon an endless expanse of water aboard a small sailboat, I try to let go of a futile search. My decades-long quest for information regarding my long-deceased Mother always seemed to end at the intersection of nowhere and nothing, where tiny glimmers of optimism evaporate into sinister disappointments that seem to enjoy my pain.

I finally accepted that any lingering shreds of evidence regarding her would require divine intervention to parse together. Like her cremated ashes, verification of any misplaced traces and places was riding the wind beyond the unknown. The search had me chasing all my yesterdays with little regard for tomorrow. My foster mothers tried to tell me what happened, but the story changed with each guardian. Soon, I stopped asking people for faulty, well-meaning, or wholly created facts. Perhaps it is time to accept a truce between the mystery surrounding my Mother's death and the hole the endeavor has left in my soul.

So, it was the brightest kind of ironic when, moments later, my Mother, after her death, indeed found me. It was unlike any childhood fairy tale I had heard while growing up, where the heroine dies decades before her story begins.

"Cindy, it looks like you have an email message," a familiar male voice interposed. "We are still close enough to civilization to get reception here."

"Only technology could be so heartless to offload

work issues upon Heaven," I replied. I knew the message had to be work-related. I have no family or husband, and I readily acknowledge that my parenting skills would have been suboptimal.

"It's Jonathan," Antonio said. "He says this is something you will want to know now."

Antonio Peterson is an experienced sailor (and physician) familiar with the Bahama area. *Chasing Hope* is a sloop he borrowed from a friend in Florida and planned to return in a few more days. But he did not cave to the usual social expectations of a physician - or fashion, for that matter. Instead, he wore a clean but somewhat tattered cotton shirt unbuttoned and fluttering in the breeze. This was "complimented" by faded polka dot shorts held up with a long piece of twine and tied into a bow.

Antonio Peterson is more than just a sailor and a physician. He is also an extraordinary person who lives for, with, and among all concerns regarding public health and the indigent. He is a master at coordinating sparse resources to help the neediest while providing ample doses of hope, help, and humanity to all at his free medical clinic. He heals souls, communicates via compassion, and is always ready to toss a lifeline to those adrift in a sea of hopelessness.

I met him by chance a year ago in the tourist part of St. Augustine (while secretly playing hooky from work). I was attending to a carriage horse vs. pedestrian accident in the street directly and suddenly before me. Within seconds, Antonio appeared in running gear from nowhere and started to help. We got the homeless victim the immediate and longer-term medical attention he needed at a nearby hospital.

This encounter led to a soul-bonding friendship, my part-time volunteer work at Antonio's free clinic, and eventually to meeting his Uncle, Jonathan Krandel Peterson, Jr. To this day, I am amazed by dear Dr. Antonio Peterson daily.

Jonathan Krandel Peterson, Jr., is a retired veterinarian and Antonio's aging Uncle. He had worked for years in the Tampa Beach area before recently retiring. Antonio is about 20 years younger, but he and Jonathan are long-time pals. They both live in DeLand, Florida. It is the same quaint historic town my Mother lived in and is about midway between Daytona Beach and Orlando, Florida. Antonio's free medical clinic is nearby – just west of the DeLand city limits.

Uncle Jonathan is also the saint looking after my sole surviving cat, Lazlo, at my home outside of DeLand during my Caribbean escape. My three other rescue cats passed away of advanced age at different times throughout the previous year. This left my younger and playful Lazlo quite lonely. Jonathan's home is five miles from mine. To make things more complicated, my last name (like Jonathan and Antonio) is Peterson also – and figuring out why has consumed many sleepless nights.

So – and not remotely reluctantly, I immediately broke two "Sailing Rules" intentionally made to prevent reality from invading paradise during our sailing adventure. Rule #1 - Wait a day before reading any text. Rule #2 – Wait another day before responding. I grabbed the cell phone. The text read: **Cindy - Important stuff! Please read.**

I found a book your mother gave me the night she was attacked in 1962. She was crying and very upset. I offered to call the police and take her to the hospital. She begged me not to do that and threatened to leave if I did. Then, she gave me a book and asked that I hang onto it for her. I tossed it into the footlocker. I knew it would be safe there and would not lose it. I was packing that footlocker in preparation to return to college early in the morning and returned my immediate attention to her. She told me she was leaving to stay with some family in the morning. Eventually, the book made it to the bottom of my footlocker. I never gave it another thought and forgot about it. It looks like her handwritten diary. Would you like it? Looks like I was right about not losing it! I apologize for it. It was still in the footlocker and the hallway closet many years later. Jonathan

I broke Rule #2 and immediately called Jonathan on the same cell phone. Before he finished saying, "Hey, Cindy," I asked questions. "Really? What does it say? Can you scan it and send me the file? Like right now?"

Jonathan said when he had a chance, "Cindy, this is

something for you to spend some time with and read, not me. I can tell you this looks to start in 1956, and the last entry is probably just before she left town. There are a few drawings here and there.

"Take your time coming home. The book is waiting on my dining room table for you. You know how to get into my house if I am not there.

"Sophie was distraught when she came over late that night. I was very concerned about her. At the time, I was packing my footlocker to return to college in the early morning. I thought that was the safest and quickest place to put the book. I never read or thought more about it, and Sophie never returned to retrieve it. And I had no idea it was a diary. I am so sorry it has taken so long to get this to you. My granddaughter asked for the footlocker to store her legions of old sheet music. That is when I found it – lying at the bottom of an old footlocker in a forgotten closet just waiting to be found."

Then Jonathan finished with, "And, about your cat – Lazlo. I think he misses you!"

After completing the call, I told Antonio, "This has been a magical trip. It exceeded my expectations and my imagination – in many, many regards. You made me feel like the most pampered and beloved princess ever. Thank you, thank you ever so very much."

"Buuuut?" Antonio asked.

"Is there any chance there is a fire-breathing, turbocharged, fully functional V-8 engine in this slow-moving sloth of a sloop somewhere?"

In a feigned British accent, Antonio said, "But of course, your Royal Highness!" He bowed and presented me with a paddle.

And so, it began...

My Mother and her diary would have to wait for our return to Florida and then DeLand – which currently felt like years and a million miles away. I needed to settle the thoughts and images flooding my brain. I tried to be cautious with the ample, familiar, and common fleeting abundance of optimism and hope – stirred together with a bit of apprehension and decades of ample chronic defeat.

Antonio and I had been sailing the Bahamas for the past ten days aboard *Chasing Hope*. We each needed time "away" and visited remote islands, some uninhabited or only existing during low tide and where we shared time and space only with birds and crabs. At one of the larger islands, I rented some jet skis, and we also did some snorkeling and fishing. We slept in a hammock on the deck beneath a blanket of celestial diamonds and lullabies of seagulls upon a gentle ocean breeze as waves lapped a nearby shore and the sun melted into splendid glory. We spent time with island folks and shared tales, rum, music, campfires, conch, fish, and coconuts to escape our version of reality and immerse our souls in just living.

I slept until the sun woke me, soaked in warm seawater, roamed new places, and explored different food, sites, people, shops, and businesses. Then, the lack of overhead power lines invited me to assemble the creatively pathetic kite to fly off the sloop as the empty spaces of freedom begged to be celebrated and touched.

The cell phone was only checked for messages when we were near an island with trappings of the 21st century. Otherwise, we bet on how long we could go without seeing a cruise ship or a car. We sang songs by Jimmy Buffet out loud (very loudly) at every opportunity. We had let all our cares and worries be carried off upon the ocean breeze and immersed ourselves in endless unrestrained freedom. We were safely secluded beyond the constant rude disruption of technology.

We both knew it could not go on forever – but at least we got to touch that possible alternate universe until our multitude of competing priorities were placed back into our ordinary madness of disorder. Up until this moment, very little could change my mindset until we arrived back in port and accepted the reality of the impossible, endless medical challenges of helping people who are experiencing poverty and unhelpfulness. But all this calm was abruptly short-circuited as my growing obsession was to get home and see what mysteries my Mother's diary could resolve for me.

My Mother, Sophie Sherman Peterson, was 16 when she died days after my birth, away from her home, alone, and with only a dubious and never-found husband on her hospital admission record. I knew of her Father and Mother, my grandparents Walters and Camille Sherman. According to my Case Manager and Inheritance Manager, both were the only children of their family to survive World War II and illness into adulthood. Furthermore, no surviving aunts, uncles, cousins, or grandparents of my mother were found.

Sophie was the lone crusader left to carry on a wealthy family name and the work, memories, legacies, traditions, and past generations of stories.

Walters Sherman (Sophie's Father) was a self-made man without a college education. Still, his bank account profited generously from several beneficial post-World War II business deals adjoining opportunities with connections. Being the only family survivor, a notice of a considerable inheritance came my way after his death. I was nine years old at the time. It came from a grandfather I had never met and piled guilt upon an endless heap of confusion.

With just bits and pieces of fact, I assume I am from this planet. As a child, I grew up parentless and became quite disenchanted with the typical fairytales of happily ever after. My desire for a stable home of marginal comfort and genuine concern among dozens of foster caregivers undoubtedly influenced this. I long felt as if my past had evaporated into oblivion. I had come from nowhere and was headed in the same direction with my single suitcase containing all my worldly possessions. There is nothing like nothing to make you long to appreciate something.

Additionally, being unable to find living relatives anywhere on the globe, I appeared to be the last of this line of Sherman – unless I could determine who my Father was. So, I searched for him without other family tree branches to explore. On my Mother's final hospitalization record, and before she lapsed into a coma, there was mention of Randal Peterson being her husband – my potential Father – and hence my last name of Peterson. Unfortunately, the name had no documentation, leads, or outcome until I serendipitously encountered Jonathan Peterson about a year ago. The very same cat-sitting Jonathan who recently discovered the diary of my Mother and the Uncle of my friend, coworker, and current Captain of *Chasing Hope* - Antonio Peterson.

At 18, I joined the Army. My years there gave me the education and skills to become a Physician Assistant (PA). However, while working in civilian hospitals, I became disenchanted with the perverse incentives of income-oriented healthcare. To me, "Health Scare & Repair" became feeble attempts to manage impossible social problems impacting health and beat caring people into zombies who became blinded to the plight of others. This was not the dream of helping others I fell in love with while in college. Healthcare increasingly supported an ever-growing bureaucracy rather than humanity needing help.

Fortunately, my penchant for computer technology qualified me for a job in nearby Sanford, Florida, managing healthcare data and analytics. I do that for a living today, but Antonio convinced me to volunteer at his free clinic on weekends. My previous military experience provided ample experience patching up soldiers and civilians. At his clinic, I again found a renewed joy and humanity within patient care, along with creative solutions for an overlooked yet very appreciative community of the working poor. In the process, Dr. Peterson (alias Antonio) became my very best friend.

While working with him in his clinic, I mentioned I had come to DeLand to finally settle my grandfather's estate and continue an unsuccessful search for Randal Peterson – my supposed Father. As a result, Antonio arranged for me to meet his Uncle Jonathan at a Thanksgiving dinner last year at the beachside home of his mother, Gloria. After the meal, Jonathan asked to talk with me on the back porch. Once there, Jonathan provided me with many answers and many more questions.

THERE ONCE WAS A GIRL NAMED SOPHIE

Jonathan said with a slightly crooked smile, "Antonio's Father is Edgar Peterson, Jr. He was born in 1935 and was named after our Grandfather. I am Edgar's younger brother. I was born in 1941. I was named Jonathan Krandel Peterson, Jr. after our Father, Jonathan Krandel Peterson, Sr. So, my older brother was named after our Grandfather. I came along later and was named after my Father. It is not the typical way to assign Jr. and Sr. to sons – but whatever.

"To avoid the same first name confusion with my Father and wanting to dodge that awful middle name of Krandel, I was often called Randal or Randy until after I graduated from college. However, I did live next door to Sophie Sherman, your Mother, until she was about 12 years old, and then I would come back home between the college terms or holidays for a few days," he explained.

An official record search showed that Jonathan Peterson, Jr. lived next door to Sophie Sherman in DeLand. However, he "moved out of town to college" long before her death. His unrecorded nickname, Randal Peterson, is likely the person on Mother's hospital record. However, my joy at thinking I had finally found my Father in Jonathan, alias the elusive Randal, was short-lived.

Jonathan remembered her fondly as a bright girl interested in plants and animals. Her Father, Walters, was not the most pleasant chap, but she appeared well cared for. Unfortunately, her mother died when Sophie was quite young.

"In short, she and I were friends – but there was no way I am your Father or her husband. I understand she passed away shortly after giving birth to you. For that, I am immeasurably sorry. She would have been a fabulous mother." I recall him saying.

"I was several years older and was away at college for her pre and early teenage years. I first entered college when I was 17 years old. If I recall correctly, the last time I saw her was when I was preparing to return to college after a short visit to my parent's home. It was late June 1962. It was a few months after her 15th birthday, and I would have been approaching 21 then." He paused a moment,

"Cindy, I am happy to have DNA testing performed if that makes you more comfortable."

I shook my head no. I was so accustomed to dead ends, and this would be another disappointment. And no, nothing that might jeopardize my present friendship with Anthony or Jonathan was worth it. Not even for my primary mission and obsession in life for the past several decades.

"Sophie told me late that evening that she had been "bothered" by a few boys. I thought she said they were teenage boys - but I don't recall her exact description. She managed to get away and run home. There she was beaten by her Father - your delightful grandfather, Walters. She told me she planned to leave and stay with other family members. I offered to call the police and take her to the hospital. She refused. She was afraid her Father would hurt her more. She was crying. Remember, there were limited to no child protection teams to call then. I gave her a suitcase and the money I had from selling my old guitar that day. I told my parents about her situation in the early morning. We did check on her that morning before leaving for college.

"She and the puppy I had given her for her 15th birthday and her car were gone.

"Perhaps Sophie used my name as a husband because she could think of no other trusted person. Maybe she was afraid Walters would find and hurt her," he said.

"Only, Jonathan, she had no other family to go to. Not anywhere. She had no grandparents, aunts, uncles, cousins, no one who could be considered family," I said.

"I did not realize that, but she never mentioned other family members. When my Father asked Walters about Sophie, he said she had gone away to school. My parents had already sold their house, and within a few days of her disappearance, they moved to Tallahassee. After that, I lost all contact with Sophie," Jonathan replied.

"Cindy, I wish my family and I had known the truth about what happened to Sophie because we would have found a way to help her. And I am so immeasurably sorry for the circumstances you grew up in," he said.

Jonathan gently opened his wallet and said, "She would want you to have this. I took this picture of Sophie on her 15th birthday with a puppy I had given her. I took several pictures of her and Winslow that day, but I made a small extra copy of this shot to keep for myself and in my wallet. It has been there ever since then." He handed me a small, old black-and-white photograph of a young girl with an adorable white puppy. They each had the same hint of an eternal similar smile.

"Sophie named her puppy Winslow – the same name she said she wanted for her daughter someday," he told me. Jonathan also told me stories about her chasing fireflies just after sunset, planting gardens of wildflowers and vegetables, and babysitting his young cousin, Antonio - alias the present-day Dr. Antonio Peterson.

"Jonathan, you just gave me the most precious gift I could ever imagine," I replied. I finally had tangible proof of my Mother from someone who knew her.

Fast forwarding to today - in my possession is that same black-and-white photograph of my Mother on her 15th birthday. I wonder if she had any indication that everything in her life was about to change radically. Of course, real life excels at destroying the dreams held by mere mortals, but how did an intelligent child of wealthy parentage end up alone and dying so young and away from home? Who was my mother? What was she like? That was the story I sought.

Sophie Sherman, 15th birthday

https://pixabay.com/photos/puppy-young-lady-kiss-kisses-2681767/

Image by JackieLou DL from Pixabay

The gentle yet almost haunting determination in her eyes impressed me as someone trapped within a binary black-and-white world and searching for one of adventure. The puppy appears to have found her soul mate.

Once again, I felt I was the strangest outcast in yet a stranger world. She resembled a comforting apparition that visits me in times of trouble. And I questioned why time and place had separated the most important person from my side and my life.

I put a copy of her photograph on Facebook and asked what others could recall of her. Responses came from local DeLand people in their late 60s to age 85. Memories included her Father attending town and board meetings and suspicion of him killing his wife, Camille, and Sophie. There were many fond memories of Sophie being a kind, pretty, polite, brilliant girl whose wealthy Father had sent her away to private school when she was about 15. No one ever heard from her again.

SAILING HOME – (PAINFULLY SLOWLY)

As we had a few quiet days of sailing before getting back home, I reviewed on a broader scale, once again, what I knew of DeLand, Florida, my Mother, and her situation:

DeLand, Florida, was founded in 1882 by Henry DeLand, a prominent businessman from New York. Mr. DeLand was instrumental in marketing orange groves to northerners longing to escape the cold weather. He also provided the young city with churches, a school, and his wealthy contacts – such as John B. Stetson.

Today, the city continues to retain a significant amount of historical significance. It was, and still is, the home to Stetson University, many historic buildings, a quaint downtown area of diverse businesses and restaurants, the wonderful, celebrated Athens Theater, sidewalks, beautiful trees, and a yearly fabulous Dog Parade through downtown. In addition, it is believed to be the first city in Florida to have electricity – thanks to an acquaintance of John B. Stetson named Thomas Edison.

DeLand recently earned the title of Tree City USA for the 30th consecutive year. A tour around town readily shows how this was well-earned. The love of trees allegedly dates to 1886, when residents were offered 50 cents off their taxes for each oak tree they planted, provided it lived one year. So many trees were planted that the city soon repealed the tax break.

I have searched various county birth records and found Walters Sherman, Sophie's Father (and my grandfather), was born October 2, 1922, in New York. Per United States records, Walters never served in the military because of his "flat feet" and being the only surviving male (and only) child. However, some early City Commission records indicate he helped his Father broker supply and manufacturing deals with the US Army in the late 1930s.

In his earlier adult years, Walters gained significant prominence in the DeLand community. He was often mentioned in the local newspaper and served on various boards of business and political interest. He lived in a large two-story Mediterranean revival house of historical status today near the 300 block of West Minnesota Avenue. (The address number has changed a few times over the decades because of the initiation of zip codes and 9-1-1.)

Among the small items removed from Walters' home and stored for me was one framed letter from Princeton University on April 23, 1962. It provided Sophie Sherman with a four-year scholarship upon graduating high school. According to the date on the letter, she was 15 years of age at the time.

I still understand little regarding the details leading up to my birth when my Mother was 16 years old. I know only that Sophie (my Mother) was in Ocala, Florida, at the time, about 60 miles northwest of

DeLand. I do not know how she got there, why she left home or was alone and destitute then.

The only information I received regarding my Mother from the Foster Home Association was my birth certificate so I could join the Army. At the time, I guessed that simply being alive and present was not proof enough of being born and currently alive.

After what feels like an eternity of looking, I now accept that Randal Peterson, the name mentioned as her possible husband and my Father, is indeed the present-day Jonathan Peterson – and he is not her husband or my Father.

After twenty years in the Army, I left and returned to the DeLand to finally settle Grandad's estate and sell some other acreage he owned. It took longer than I expected. So, I sold my house about 30 miles away on the county's east side and bought a three-bedroom home just west of DeLand on half an acre recently. It makes traveling to volunteer at the nearby free clinic with Antonio on weekends much easier. In addition, the driving time to my weekday analytics job in Sanford is much quicker than when my home was in Port Orange.

According to Randal, Sophie Sherman (my Mother) grew up as a bright, adventurous young lady in a wealthy family in DeLand, Florida, from the late 1940s to the early 1960s. Various records and school yearbooks confirm that Sophie Sherman indeed lived there.

FAMILY DOCUMENTS

From the information on my birth certificate, I could find the location of the apartment building where Sophie (my Mother) and I were living. The building was bulldozed days after Sophie's death. The Ocala, Florida, hospital where my Mother died no longer exists. Finding evidence of my Mother's life has been a challenge. Below is what I have been able to find through years of searching. While it is a good start, it leaves many more questions.

Documents I have included:

• **Emergency Room Notes, Ocala, Florida - March 30, 1963** – A young adult female was found in a semi-conscious state at the bottom of stairs in a condemned building. She is lethargic and says, "Sharleen," and arrives via ambulance at the hospital, injured and with an elevated temperature. She is found to be post-partum and possibly septic with a severe head injury post-fall. Her driver's license, in her pocket, indicates her name is Sophie Sherman. She does respond when called "Sophie." A small, cracked mirror is in her pocket, which likely broke during her fall.

When asked about a baby, she nods yes. Police are sent to the scene to search for an infant. The infant was found upstairs in the same building and brought to the hospital with a tattered rag doll and a small towel with SM or WS (depending on which it faced) hand embroidered on it. The female infant (alias, me - Cindy) appears about two weeks old and healthy. A shoestring is tied on what is left of the umbilical cord. A Nurse placed the baby beside her Mother about 45 minutes before Sophie succumbed to her injuries.

Before her death, Sophie mentions a possible husband named Randal Peterson. This person is not found locally. Information from her driver's license is used to locate Sophie's Father, Walters Sherman, in DeLand, Florida. He admits to Sophie being his daughter but refuses to consent to treatment. He does not know her current age (16 is indicated on the driver's license) or any past medical history regarding her. He would not provide information regarding anyone named Randal Peterson or Sharleen and declined to accept care of the infant. He was informed of the critical condition of Sophie, and for next of kin purposes, a death certificate for Sophie and a birth certificate for the baby will likely be sent to him via mail. He provided his attorney's name and phone number and hung up the telephone.

For temporary identification purposes, the infant (myself) is named Cindy (by nursing staff after "Cinderella" according to the nursing notes) Peterson (anticipating the location of the Father). No Randy or Randal Peterson of 18 to 35 years of age is readily found in Ocala, Florida – other than one currently enlisted in Military Service and has been out of the country for the past two years. Shortly after, Sophie became unresponsive, experienced a grand mal seizure, and passed away.

- **Sophie's Death Certificate** – March 30, 1963.

Cause of death: Skull fracture secondary to fall and septicemia. Remains are cremated, uncollected by Walters Sherman, and disposed of. Randal Peterson, as a possible husband, is not found.

- **Coroner Report** - April 2, 1963. This female appears to be the listed age of 16 years. Injury of bruising and abrasions are consistent with an unwitnessed apparent fall on wooden stairs and a concrete landing. The evident head injury is consistent with x-ray findings of frontal skull fracture and local hemorrhage. Medics at the scene stated the stairs were in poor repair. There is no indication of violence. An incidental finding of a small, irregular birthmark is found on the anterior upper right thigh, not associated with trauma. The patient is postpartum approximately two weeks.

- **Birth Certificate of Cindy Peterson (Me!)** - March 14 (estimated), 1963. Unattended birth. Birthplace unknown, date unknown, time unknown, and birth weight unknown. Mother- Sophie Sherman (Peterson). Age - 16 years.

- **Child Placement** - April 4, 1963. Determines Walters Sherman is unfit to care for the infant and refuses to allow adoption. I (Cindy) went to various foster homes until I joined the military at age 18 and became a Physician Assistant.

- **Other documents I have been able to locate include**:

- **Birth Certificate of Walters Sherman** - October 2, 1922. Father of Sophie Sherman. Born in New York. Per local news records, he came to DeLand, Florida, at age 6 with his Father.

- **Birth Certificate of Camille Maria Benoit** - November 1, 1925. Assumed mother of Sophie Sherman. She was born in the French quarter of New Orleans.

- **Marriage Certificate of Walters and Camille Maria Benoit** - February 14, 1946. Probable parents of Sophie Sherman.

- **Death Certificate of Walters Sherman** - July 9, 1972, at his home. Cause of death: malnutrition, debilitation, and senility.

As my Mother, Sophie, had died shortly after my birth, when Walters, my grandfather, died in 1972, I was nine years old and the lone family survivor. I was surprised to learn of my inheritance from a man I had never met.

The funds were released to me on my 25th birthday.

Despite multiple attempts, I have been unable to locate Sophie Sherman's birth certificate. She was likely an only child. No marriage certificate for her and Randal Peterson is found either.

City records indicate Walters and Sophie Sherman lived in the same home in DeLand, Florida, during the late 1940s, 50s, and early 60s. Camille Sherman was only mentioned there until early 1951. Walters remained there until his death. I have been looking for the Birth Certificate of Sophie Sherman locally or within adjacent counties. She was probably born in DeLand, FL., to Camille and Walters Sherman, likely in 1947, given her age of 16 at death in 1963.

THE DIARY

So, a whole new chapter of yet another volume of trying to find where I came from and was about to begin... again. It is a twisted irony to stumble upon the past and bring info about your long-deceased Mother into the present for the first time. How often I dreamed about her and what happened in her life. So many times, hope has been smothered before.

After sailing to the dock and returning the sloop, I was at Jonathan's home within two hours. He was not there, but my Mother's diary was on the dining room table, as he said. The afternoon sunlight from the skylight above shone directly upon its dark brown paper cover for extra dramatic effect. I briefly stood in awe, took a deep breath, and ran to wash and dry my hands before touching the history of my life.

This diary was the single most significant record of my Mother's life, and it survived untouched for over half a century. I took a moment to reflect upon the long road to get here and the series of events that brought this book before me now. It all came down to What If:

I had not played hooky from work that day, took an aimless ride with no specific destination in mind, and found myself randomly strolling through St. Augustine when,

- a car tire had exploded nearby, spooking the horse pulling a carriage and injuring a homeless man who was walking near its path and

- headed to the front of the line awaiting the fast-food restaurant post-lunch rush of "incorrect hamburger orders" to hit the dumpster, and when

- Antonio decided to take a shortcut jogging to avoid traffic a block away - just in time to encounter me tending to the injured man and

- which ultimately resulted in us becoming great friends.

Now, I can add to that scenario: And

- Jonathan's granddaughter requested the old footlocker of his college youth and "buried" within a forgotten hall closet to store her collection of sheet music, which

- Contained a long-forgotten diary my Mother requested he keep for her more than half a century ago?

In many ways, this book was a miracle and the key to solving a lifelong mystery of what happened and who my Mother was. With more than a fair amount of trepidation, I opened the front cover of a remarkably well-preserved book to see a hand-printed statement on the first inside page that stated,

"This is dedicated to my soulmate mirror image and those beyond. SS"

Already, I was in awe of the person I was about to meet.

Wanting to set aside a time and place to support my full attention, I quickly did a cursory assessment of the book. It was a standard-sized leather-bound book with a carefully hand-folded, tightly wrapped brown paper cover. Over half the pages contained dated, mostly legible handwritten printing and cursive.

It was a diary covering the last seven years of the meager 16 years my Mother was alive. I was grateful, overwhelmed, and apprehensive about what I might find. From all accounts, only she knew what had become of her life. Scant few family documents existed as many were destroyed by her Father in a backyard bonfire blaze after Sophie "disappeared," according to his neighbors. This diary was the most important document of her life and had survived since last being touched by herself and Jonathan one night in 1962.

I immediately appreciated the magnitude and wonder of the contents within this document, known only to my Mother. I suddenly became aware of the necessity to hold the book at arm's length to protect the brown paper cover from unauthorized tears rolling down my face.

Then, I heard the back door open, and Jonathan walked in.

"I am so glad you are here! Did you have a good trip?" he asked.

"It was magnificent, and this diary is beyond words. Thank you, thank you. You make miracles happen!" I said.

"I was so worried you would be mad with me for taking so long to get this to you. I had forgotten all about it. But truthfully, I had no idea it was a diary. Sophie read lots of books. I had never looked at it. I am so sorry it took so long," he replied with his head hanging a bit low. "You have every right to be angry with me."

"Jonathan, please! I am so very and eternally grateful." I applied a sincere hug, which he gratefully returned.

I sat on one of four chairs provided with the dining room table and said, "Please have a seat," behaving as if I owned the house, not him.

"Tell me more!" I said intently.

Jonathan went to the kitchen and returned with two glasses of iced tea. He pensively sat across from me at the table and told me of an extraordinary girl who lived next door to him while growing up.

"And in all seriousness, Cindy, I have no more idea about what happened to Sophie than you do. I thought it was a good idea for her to stay with family elsewhere - as she said she would do," he said.

"Please, take your time with the diary and enjoy appreciating a remarkable young lady! Let me know if I can answer any questions! It was a long time ago, but I am sure some stories are left in my old head if you can prompt them properly."

I hugged him, put the diary into a plastic bag, and headed home. Lazlo, my cat, undoubtedly thought I had abandoned him for all time by now.

As soon as possible, I found a quiet time and place, cleaned off my desk, put a clean towel atop it, and sat down to read the old but well-preserved diary.

The book was in good shape, considering the decades and Florida heat and humidity. Also, thanks to the thick paper that neatly fitted and wrapped about the entire cover and the protection afforded within a footlocker of an air-conditioned home. The book's spine had separated from the pages and was gapping slightly. Yet, somehow, it felt as if it was waiting for me as much as I was waiting for it in return.

For a moment, I was hesitant and felt I was entering my Mother's secret realm of privacy. Prying into the personal thoughts and lives of others is not something I want to do. But then, this message was found, sent, and delivered here at the right time and place to the only person in the world most anxious to read it. I was convinced she would like me to read it. She had written it for this moment in time, and finally, the treasure map to my life had arrived.

Upon opening, it was handwritten; some manuscripts are in block print, especially on the earlier pages, but most are in cursive in the later entries. As the dingy white pages progressed, pencils became fountain pens and eventually made their way into ballpoint pens. Some handwriting, especially the pencil-written entries near the beginning, could be clearer and easier to read. Some pages also contained drawings or dried flowers. Mostly pencil and black pen splayed upon the white pages of life's reality for a young girl growing up during tumultuous times.

Back to current-day reality, and despite just returning from a sailing trip through the Caribbean, I managed to beg a few more days off work to focus my attention on the diary. Thank goodness for an empathetic working partner and friend who agreed to work for me until Thursday.

THEY CALL ME SOPHIE

And finally, after more decades than I care to admit, the story of my Mother's life begins...

Friday, March 9, 1956. HELLO DIRY! They call me Sophie, *and it is my birthday! Miss Ellie gave me this book for my 9th birthday. TODAY! I so want to write in it. We will talk about school, shopping, holidays, friends, and so much more. Last year, for my birthday, she gave me a poodle skirt! I have an old picture of it that I will put into this diary. Miss Ellie is the greatest lady in the world! What is it like to be 9? Friends came over after school, and we played, danced in the yard, pinned tails on a cardboard donkey, played games, and ate cake and ice cream. This evening, Miss Ellie and I planted a small Magnolia tree in the front yard. She said the branches look like Angel wings – so she calls it the Angel Tree. She says she wants to watch both of us as we grow up! I hope this diary will be a secret place to keep my hopes, dreams, and questions. Sophie.*

Cindy – Wow! What a fabulous treat to get a glimpse of the world and a picture of your Mother when she was so young and carefree! I carefully cradled the black and white photograph of a happy girl in a poodle skirt picture in my hands. I looked into her face and smiled. I felt a wonderful relationship and adventure were about to begin.

To get into the "life" of the times, I quickly searched the Internet to find that in 1956, "Lassie" and "I Love Lucy" were the favorites on TV, and Elvis Presley was crooning out "Don't Be Cruel" over the radio waves.

Although I admit to limited experience with such things, I anticipated a nine-year-old girl to write in a diary about her random thoughts and personal perception of events. My initial impression was that the writing and ideas were of someone concerned with her world of nine years. The entries usually started with a date and sometimes ended with her name. Here, the next day, she already includes a bit of history...

Sophie *– Saturday, March 10, 1956 - I should say a bit about myself before Miss Ellie gave me this grate diry to write. I think I was born here; I remember little of my mother before the day the amblance and police came. She seemed kind but cried and yelled sometimes. One time, she threw a pot of hot water at father. He lives here with me. Sophie*

Cindy – She provides a short but interesting introduction. And Sophie also provided firsthand testimonials of the time, flora, and fauna of DeLand, FL.

Sophie *– Saturday, March 17, 1956 – I bot some milkweed with my allowance and replanted wildflowers from the field into the back garden. Also, I bot some tomato, green pepper, and watermelon seeds. I tried to plant some sunflowers – but the birds liked them too* *much. I am hoping to see Monarch butterflies again this year. It is St. Patrick's Day. Sophie*

Cindy - The entries mostly prattled about her various dolls, Lassie's television shows, the circus moving into town, and fairy tales with Prince Charming. It was written quite well for a 9-year-old. Miss Ellie is her Nanny. (Jonathan provided me with some info on this). According to her comments, Sophie appeared energetic and full of life, and she loved wildflowers, animals, school, and anything colored turquoise. She had friends and did well in school. But - some entries are a bit confusing as well...

***Sophie**- Tuesday, April 24, 1956, When we were much younger, sometimes, we had a flashlight and lit our faces in the dark. Once, I remember when Miss Ellie came into the room when she heard us giggling about dumb things a boy said in school that day. She was always watching over like a mother hen. I don't remember when Miss Ellie first came to our house to live – but it seems she has been here forever. She used to sing to me as she brushed my hair. Sometimes, she would pretend to be my Fairy Godmother and make me a tin foil crown. Sophie*

***Sophie** – Monday, April 30, 1956 – Miss Ellie took us for my yearly doctor checkup today. In the waiting room was an old Life magazine of children crossing over a bridge to the castle on the day Disneyland opened in 1955. There were pictures of people spinning in a teacup ride. It looks wonderful! We were* *late getting to school, but it was ok. I want to be a princess – with a magic wand to make everything pretty, happy, and good. Sophie.*

***Sophie** – Sunday, May 13, 1956 - I went with Mrs. Williston to the Methodist church today. I missed a couple of weeks because she was sick. I brot her some wildflowers from the yard – it is **Mother's Day!** She was so happy! I sometimes go with Miss Ellie to her church, and everyone stays in the churchyard after the service. Children play, women plan things and make food, and men talk. They make good chicken and mashed potatoes. I helped clean up a bit and played with the kids on the playground – until the boys started throwing mud pies at us girls. Sophie*

First Methodist Church DeLand, circa1950's.
Founded 1880.PR13369
https://www.floridamemory.com/items/show/ 11769

Cindy – Records show that Mrs. Williston lived next door to Sophie and her Father.

Sophie – Friday, May 18, 1956 - I learned in science today that people are animals. Really? Is that true? – because we plan, think, read, and make things more than we need. People are also artists. We have money – no dog has money or even pockets to put it in. Doesn't that make us more than animals? I learn about things in school, where Miss Ellie understands how to think. We spent years learning how to get smart like her. How can I do that?

Cindy – OK - that is a challenging question! The girl, along with being "chatty," brings up some good points! I savor each word, entry, and page and desperately worry about Sophie when she does not show up in the diary for several days. I was wondering how and why life kidnapped her away from me!

Sophie – Tuesday, June 12, 1956 – We are on summer break from school. Nancy's parents took us to see Bambi – I was the only one there not crying in the movie. I wanted to think that mother bravely died so I could somehow live – to be that speshal to her. Nancy said it was a very sad movie – poor Bambi. It was like Charlotte's Web book – where the mother dies before getting to know her children. No one should be left without a mother – thank goodness for Miss Ellie. I came home and hugged her. I wondered what would make the very best mother – what "parts" from others could I merge all together into one wonderful mother.

- *- The Wisdom of Miss Ellie*

- *- The Hope of Anne Frank*

- *- The Patience of Anne Sullivan*

- *- The Adventure of Amelia Earhart*

- *- The Love of Mother Teresa*

- *- The Encouragement of Randal*

Yup, that all describes Miss Ellie well.

And then the thunderstorm had me closing the windows. The storms are amazing to watch from the front porch. The lightning and thunder are thrilling. The gods spew searing shards upon the humbled kingdom – and Mother Nature bathed the wounds of terror with water.

Tomorrow, I plan to ride my bike to the library – at the corner of East New York and Garfield. Since the school library is closed for the summer. Me

DeLand Public Library circa 1950.PR13317
https://www.floridamemory.com/items/show/11717

Sophie – Monday, July 2, 1956 - Miss Ellie walked me to the Athens theater to see a movie. We sat on the balcony, and I brought my RC bottle caps to pay for them. At first, Miss Ellie didn't want to go inside. She is my nanny, and they know my father, so they let her in with me. She had never been there before, so I showed her around. Nancy and her parents used to take me here back in first grade. Nancy and I would have sleepovers at her house and stay up all night. Miss Ellie liked the movie. I don't recall the name of it. There was a horse in it. I bought us popcorn and Coca-Cola. Sophie

Cindy –The Athens Theater opened on January 6, 1922, in DeLand as a silent film and Vaudeville theater. Today, talented performers regularly provide live music and theater entertainment for DeLand and Central Florida residents.

Athens Theater

Cindy – As I would've expected of a nine-year-old, her early diary entries reflected the random and sometimes incomplete thoughts of someone concerned with her world.

Sophie – *Tuesday, July 24, 1956 - I told my mirror today to "Smile!" People don't see much of anything wrong when you smile, and it makes them smile back. I dreamed again last night about the day the ambulance came. It was the day you stopped crying. Please smile for me. I worry. Sophie*

Cindy - I was hoping for more explanation here, but I was so thrilled to read it and see and feel the same paper as my Mother did to ask for more. The most important person to me was sharing her world with me!

I could feel her presence within her written words and thoughts.

Sophie – *Wednesday, July 25, 1956 - I showed my Sophie rag doll that I have had forever to the mirror looking back at me. I pretended to make her talk and dance a bit. She will always be my favorite, and I will keep her forever and ever. I sometimes wonder if I exist and if anyone sees me. Then I look in the mirror and realize I am not alone, and I look back and smile at you. There you are, waiting for me - and me for you. S*

Cindy – Days and sometimes weeks would go by without an entry from Sophie. Other times, they were simply snippets of words... "Get up. Go to school. Nothing special." "Church with Miss Ellie," "Piano practice is ok. My piano teacher, Miss Lewis, told me to think of the piano keyboard as a range of colors combined at different moments in time. Create a glorious picture throughout the air with music."

Other entries showed me the world surrounding her - "The azaleas are blooming, and the place is gorgeous." "Going to the recital." "Got green beans from my garden." "Elvis Presley – sings really well. Nancy and Sue like to dance to it! Nancy says it razzes her berries!"

Throughout it, there were mentions of gentle transitions through seasons and subtle words about the foliage, holidays, etc. Later, it took me a moment to figure it out, "Get up. Go to school. Nothing special" became "Gu. Gts. Ns."

Cindy – She also wrote quite a bit about personal things and TV shows. She liked "Alfred Hitchcock Presents" (I was surprised – she seems to enjoy suspense), and Miss Ellie saw her daily "stories" such as "Search for Tomorrow" and "The Secret Storm." She complained that toys for boys were more interesting than the ones for girls. She wanted an accordion or models to build. She mentioned visiting with her reflection in the mirror. She wrote about friends and shopping and seems to like nature topics regarding plants and animals. At one point, Miss Ellie took her to buy some shoes for gym class and running.

Sophie mentions talking with Mrs. Williston (the old lady next door who keeps hard-boiled eggs in her refrigerator door. She draws a smiley face on each with a pencil.) I asked her about it – she said anything to keep me from being sad and lonely, and her dog, a brown dachshund (or wiener dog as Sophie calls it) named Sinatra, goes for walks through the neighborhood. Sinatra howls (some say he sings) to the church bells each week. Many neighbors would come from their front porches to talk with Sophie along the way. She also loved banana chocolate malts from McCrory's and Woolworth's in downtown DeLand. From the writing style of a nine-year-old, she appeared talkative and anxious to meet everyone.

Cindy - I phoned Jonathan yesterday, Saturday, during a quiet afternoon in Antonio's free clinic, where I sometimes volunteer. I told him about the diary entries and some things I read. I mentioned that Sophie often talked with her mirror – which, while I suppose is not too uncommon, her entries seemed to take the self-conversations further.

He thought momentarily as if he appeared to pass judgment on a decision. "Cindy," he said. "Let's find a quiet place to sit and talk a bit. There is something I need to tell you."

Not seeing an abundance of urgency in the request, I asked him to come and see me tomorrow. Besides, Lazlo would be thrilled to see him again.

"No, the sooner, the better. How about we meet up at our usual place in Sherman Park? Can you go when you are done at the clinic?" Jonathan was a bit anxious.

"Sure. I'll see you there at about 4:15," I replied.

RELATIVE REFLECTION

The breeze was gentle, birds happily chattered, and kids played. Sherman Park was built with the guilt money from my inheritance. It is an excellent park for the residents to relax and enjoy nature, kids on the playground, and a community center for meetings. It is also where Antonio and I meet weekly on Wednesday early evenings to catch up on things and relax a bit. On occasion, his Uncle Jonathan joins us as well. Jonathan awaited me at the usual picnic table under a giant oak tree. After the common hugs, smiles, and brief updates, he jumped right into what he had to say.

"Cindy, thanks for coming. Are you enjoying the diary?" he asked.

"Jonathan, it is perhaps the most astounding thing I have ever read. I am trying to take it slowly, but I am also very anxious to read as fast as possible. So, I try to pace myself and remember that it took her six-plus years to write it.

"I recall there are several things you might appreciate. You may find some of it interesting – but perhaps not happy. Nonetheless, it would help if you heard this from me first. For example – Sophie did have a sister," he said.

I took a deep, unexpected breath. **"I have an aunt! How did I manage to miss that?"** I was shocked.

He said, "Well, you had good reason to miss it. I never explored whether Sophie knew she had a sister. Her sister died at a very young age. They were identical twins. It was something we did not talk about with her. No one would. It was bad enough that she lost her mother. It was a code of silence from all who tried to "protect" her from the harsh reality of some truth. It was a long time ago, but it seems her sister's name was Sharlene, something close to that," he said.

"Cindy, her sister, was not quite four years old when allegedly, her mother, Camille, pushed her sister down the stairs into the basement of her house. She died at the bottom of the stairs. I was about ten years old then, and my parents would not tell me much about it. But, on "the day the ambulance came" – a phrase you might hear from the neighbors, I saw a police car and an ambulance at her home. The ambulance took away her mother, Camille, and Sophie's sister, Sharlene (I don't know how it was spelled), who had died. Neither were ever seen here again, nor was there a funeral for either. Although, as I recall, I heard your grandmother, Camille, yelling something about "the devil." She was very agitated, screaming, and it took two men to get her into the ambulance," Jonathan said.

"Soon after that, a Nanny named Miss Ellie moved in to care for Sophie. I met her a few times. That lady was the kindest, most gentle, and wisest soul. Sophie would tell me often about how much she loved her."

"I am only in the first year of her diary, which starts on her ninth birthday, but she does mention Miss Ellie," I said.

"If I understand correctly, Sophie's mother, Camille, was suspected of having something to do with the death of Sophie's sister. I assumed Camille went to an out-of-town hospital to keep down the neighborhood gossip. But a little over a year later, information was printed in the local newspaper that Camille Sherman had died of pneumonia in Florida State Hospital up north."

He paused for a moment.

"That facility provided care and incarceration for patients with serious mental illness issues. I recall my parents being concerned about Camille's ability to cope with two infants and your grandfather's busy and often absent professional life punctuated with occasional bouts of moderate drinking. Then, of course, all kinds of stories were going around town. Regardless, Sophie was a great kid. She was brilliant, ambitious, and kind.

"And, I have no idea how much of this was ever shared with Sophie by others – or what she knew or perhaps figured out on her own. The town loved her and did everything possible to spare her pain. She was a very brave, very kind, and very smart girl. And in fairness to Walters, it likely was not easy to quell the gossip surrounding his wife's sudden departure, the death of a child, and being left with a very young daughter to raise. His public appearances slowly tapered off from that point forward."

"Sharlene?" I said. "Sophie said "Sharleen" to the Ambulance crew before she died in 1963. It was spelled S-h-a-r-l-e-e-n on her hospital notes. They thought she was just confused from the head injury."

We were quiet momentarily, both trying to process the decades of no information.

"Jonathan, thanks. This does help quite a bit with understanding some of the things she writes about. Maybe that explains her talking to her bedroom mirror. I noticed she mentions "we" now and then. Can you tell me more about Miss Ellie? Sophie loves her, but there are places Miss Ellie seems reluctant to go," I said.

"That, unfortunately, makes perfect sense for the times at least. In the 1950s and '60s, most black people were not warmly welcomed in all places. And DeLand and Volusia County, in general, had unfortunately significant history with violent Klan members," he replied.

"Wow – there is something I had not previously considered. Ellie is Black? I am not sure that Sophie sees this. However, I did skip and "fast-forwarded" through some later pages in the diary. According to some later entries, she visits Miss Ellie's church sometimes and visits with people in her community," I said.

"You might be surprised, but I'm not. Sophie was a remarkable young lady and way ahead of her time. Read more, and I have no doubt you should be prepared to be amazed. And remember, she may mention Randal or, perhaps, Randy (alias, yours truly) here and there. That is what she called me. I am not sure she ever knew my actual name, Jonathan. And – as mentioned previously, I am not her husband or your Father, but please keep me updated and let me know if you have any questions – I am glad to help where I can." He smiled.

"I cannot tell you how happy I am that this diary finally ended with you. It might be the most wonderful thing I have been able to do for anyone - ever," he said before finishing with a hug.

Armed with all this new information, I planned to go on yet another quest for a birth certificate for Sharleen, Sharlean, or Sharlene Sherman and two death certificates - one for her and the other for her mother, Camille Sherman. My previous searches for Sophie's birth certificate had never produced anything, but I will try that again.

While at it, I will also request copies of the police and ambulance records regarding the incident on the "day the ambulance came" - the same day her sister died in her home. Experience has taught me to keep my hopes subdued. The offices are open on Monday. In the meantime, that evening, I was anxious to read more of her diary.

Sophie – *Monday, September 10, 1956 - I found out today that Mikey in school is leaving to go to the Military school soon. His brother will go there too. It just opened a few days ago. Mikey was born a few years before me – but he seemed nice. He brought his pet hamster to school last year – and it got loose. Miss Smith screamed when it jumped out of her desk. Sophie*

Cindy - The Florida Military School opened at the old DeLand Naval Air Station facility, north of DeLand, from September 1956 until 1971. The area is now the DeLand Municipal Airport, an uncontrolled general aviation airport for recreational flying, skydiving, and special events. The City of DeLand built it in the 1920s, and the city donated it for use by the U.S. Navy in 1941. The Navy purchased more nearby property, and the DeLand Naval Air Station opened in November 1942. During World War II, it was a significant training base for Navy pilot/gunner teams. Today, it is also home to the Naval Air Museum.

Sophie – *Tuesday, October 9, 1956 - A rainbow was in my vanity mirror near my bedroom window. My room is on the second floor and above most of the trees in the yard. Outside the front window, the Magnolia tree in the front yard was starting to make its way to reach something closer to the sky. Miss Ellie says that rainbows are a postcard from God. It is a message he sends that he hasn't forgotten you. It is a small gift of kindness and joy just for you. It makes me wonder if God is really a girl. Sophie*

Sophie – On Friday, Oct 19, 1956, A big storm flooded some garden areas and dropped twigs and a few palm fronds. A window in the school got broken, and some books were wet. Some big trees fell near Woodland Blvd. Sophie

Cindy – An unnamed tropical storm did come through town on October 19, 1956, with a 40-mile-per-hour wind. In addition, the Clyde Beatty-Cole Brothers Circus moved outside of DeLand near the train station at about the same time.

Sophie – Friday, November 2, 1956. The Volusia County Fair is finally open today! It has livestock, canning, crafts, and some great rides. Millie, her little sister, and I are going with her parents on Saturday night. It is open until Nov 12th. I want some cotton candy... blue! Sophie

Today, I asked Miss Ellie the difference between an "itch" and a "scratch." Do you scratch an itch or itch a scratch? She said, "Oh, Lawd! Why do you hurt your brain with such questions?" I thought about it some more, and scratch could be a verb or a noun, but itch - I am not sure what that is. I guess you could scratch a scratch or maybe itch an itch. English is just so confusing sometimes. Me again

Sophie – Saturday, Nov 3, 1956, Wizard of Oz is on TV today! CBS. I saw it in the movie with Millie from school and her mother. I can't wait to see it on TV! I love the Scarecrow – he is so smart not to have a brain! And Toto! SS

Sophie – *Sunday, Nov 4, 1956, went to the Volusia County Fair again! Went with a couple of kids from church. I enjoyed the cows and goats – and the roosters were LOUD. I had some great pumpkin pie and hot chocolate. It would be great to have a pet goat – but it would probably eat my vegetable and flower gardens. The sites from on top of the Ferris wheel were grand. I also went into the Mirrors Fun House. Wow! Unlike the vanity mirror, I can see how much we have grown! Sophie.*

Cindy – The Volusia County Fairgrounds expanded and is currently located east of DeLand. The previous location was on W. New York Ave. The Fair is each year in November, and other events are there throughout the year.

Sophie - *Saturday, Nov 17, 1956. Miss Ellie and I went to the new Winn-Dixie to buy some food to make dinner for the poor people's shelter with her church. They make Thanksgiving dinner for those with no families or money. Sophie*

Winn-Dixie, DeLand, Florida, *circa 1956*. DOT1493
https://www.floridamemory.com/items/show/105074

Sophie - Sunday, Nov 18, 1956. There is a moon eclipse tonight. I will see if Randal has a telescope to look at it better.

Randal was away on a scouting trip with his troop. His Father said the telescope broke a few months ago when Max, Randal's dog, ran through the house one day. Dr. Peterson says he doubts it can be fixed. Max was named after the empty Maxwell House coffee can he enjoyed rolling around and down the driveway as a puppy. He is a medium-sized dog with light brownish fur with a bit of curl. We are great friends. Dr. Peterson loaned me his binoculars to see the moon tonight. Sophie

Sophie – Thursday, Nov 22, 1956, Thanksgiving Day. Getting some time off school was nice, but it was nothing special. Miss Ellie made some turkey, stuffing, and pumpkin pie yesterday. I heated them and cooked some green beans, and father and I had dinner. Afterward, I took some pie to Mrs. Williston and some turkey to Max. Both were happy about it.

Sophie *– Monday, November 26, 1956. November morning. You could tell the morning students in the class who walked or rode their bikes to school today versus those who had been driven by their family or friends or lived nearby by the cold redness at the tip of the red nose that glowed! It reminded me of Rudolph!*

Sophie *– On Saturday, December 1, 1956, Nancy and I watched the homecoming parade on Woodland Blvd. It was great, and Christmas is getting close. The Euclid High School band was in the parade in DeLand! Binoculars are OK, but I want a telescope for Christmas! Soph*

Cindy – It is worth noting that Woodland Boulevard is the main north-south road through downtown DeLand. Sometimes, the locals called it the Boulevard or Woodland, as they continue to do today.

Woodland Boulevard, DeLand, Florida image number PR13956 circa 1950
https://www.floridamemory.com/items/show/12289

Sophie – *Day Dec 25, 1956. There was a new bike from father for Christmas! It is blue, with a big red bow and a basket on the front bars for my books and things. You would LOVE it! My old bike is quite rusty and too small to be comfortable. The basket will come in handy! I hugged father. Miss Ellie seems pleased, too. I asked Miss Ellie if she knew anyone who would like my old bike. She will find a good child for it. I will clean it up nicely!*

Cindy – Throughout the years, I have found and collected scant newspaper mentions about my grandfather, Walters. In short, I surmised that Walters had sufficient local influence to make "things" happen.

I spent Monday morning at the county offices searching through large, old heaps of disordered, neglected, and tattered paper records. Today, a few county staff members need help getting current records from three years ago into a less-than-current or consistently cooperative automated record device. The documents from decades ago were not a priority. Also, as Sherman was a common last name at that time and Sharlene passed away so young, there were no documents or school papers with the proper spelling of her name. After a few attempts (Sharlene, Sharleen, and Sharlean did not bring up anything), finally, in desperation, I looked for a spelling variation I had not considered previously – Sharline.

I found a tattered **Birth Certificate** stating **Sharline Ivy Sherman** was born to **Camille and Walters Sherman** at 5:07 pm on March 9, 1947, at DeLand Memorial Hospital on North Stone Street in DeLand, Florida. Her weight was 4 pounds, 10 ounces. This original document was crumpled, written in faded fountain pen, and missing nearly half the form and blank spaces. It was not in the best, but of what was there, no mention of a twin sister is found. I was happy anyway and obtained a photocopy of it.

The certificate did show Camille, Mother, was a homemaker, and Walters, Father, was a businessman. They lived on West Minnesota Avenue. From the map of the time, it was about two blocks west of the entrance of John B. Stetson University.

In the late 1940s, DeLand was a small town of about 7,000 people trying to recover from the leftover challenges and economic, social, and mental damage inflicted by WWII. Sophie and Sharline were early post-war Baby Boomers.

Despite trying many times previously, I decided to try again to locate the birth certificate of my Mother, Sophie. I had likewise varied Sophie's spelling during a previous search for her birth certificate a few years ago but tried again anyway. Again, I looked for Sofi, Sophia, Sofie, Sofy, Sofee, and Sophie – and again without finding what I was looking for. And, unlike Sharline, there is evidence that Sophie did spell her name as S-o-p-h-i-e. Hospital records at the time of her death, high school yearbook listing from the local historical society, this diary, and comments from Jonathan and more – all agreed on that spelling.

When Sharline and assuming, Sophie were born, the DeLand Memorial Hospital was too small for the growing population and about to close and move. Perhaps that contributed to Sophie's missing birth certificate. The hospital was built in the early 1920s. Today, it is a local history museum with a 1920s operating room, an apothecary exhibit, and military and other memorabilia. It was added to the U.S. National Register of Historic Places in 1989.

***DeLand Memorial Hospital**, circa 1940s*
N029984
https://www.floridamemory.com/items/show/139565

Next, I searched for the **Death Certificates** of Sharline and Camille Sherman. As Camille Sherman had died in a hospital in another county, I had to request a copy of her certificate online. Once funding is confirmed, a copy of it will be emailed to me.

Now that I had the proper spelling of her first name on her Birth Certificate, finding the **Death Certificate** for **Sharline Sherman** was quick. A copy of the Death Certificate was found but in worse condition than her birth certificate. She was two weeks shy of four years old when she died at home on February 23, 1951, at approximately 4:30 p.m. No middle name is included on this certificate. The cause of death is listed simply as "fall downstairs." Nearly half the form is missing. I requested and was given a photocopy of the certificate.

Since I had Sharline's date of death, I also had the date "the ambulance came," – which was the same date as her mother's admission to the hospital.

I stopped for a moment, leaned back into the chair, took a deep breath, and wondered about the mayhem of that day and the everyday environment these two young girls within a family of wealth and privilege endured at the hands of Camille, a woman who became, and perhaps previously was, insane. Something was unsettled, and it felt like it needed to be placed in order within the kingdom of Sophie and Sharline.

Despite knowing her name and the date of hospital admission for Camille Sherman, I doubted I could quickly obtain a copy of her records. Of course, I could argue that I was the last surviving next of kin, but being psychiatric records, the amount of time and changes to the hospital structure and ownership over the years would make it challenging. And truthfully, any patient information it contained would likely be more "nosey" than helpful regarding Sophie. But when I found a site online to request a copy of a death certificate, I readily did so.

Next, I focused on obtaining the Police and Ambulance records of February 23, 1951, "the day the ambulance came." I contacted County Records to request the process of researching ambulance and police reports regarding the incident of that date.

I was asked to wear cotton gloves as I carefully reviewed three-ring binders of date-sorted pages containing handwritten, aging original police and ambulance paperwork. I found straps of paper indicating several pages had been torn out of the notebook. The missing documents included the date of February 23, 1951, in both the police and ambulance response notebooks of records. I silently congratulated myself on predicting Walters' ability to impact the disappearance of such things within his business, political, and personal circles.

When I arrived home, I found my computer had kindly anticipated my arrival – with an email containing an attached document of Camille Sherman's death certificate. Apparently, Walters's "power" did not extend to a hospital in northern Florida.

About 15 months after "the day the ambulance came" to the home of Sophie and Sharline Sherman, Camille Maria Benoit Sherman died on June 2, 1952, at the age indicated of "Unknown," at Florida State Hospital in Chattahoochee. The cause of death was listed simply as Pneumonia – just as Jonathan had told me. Walters Sherman was listed as her estranged husband. Sophie was five years old when her mother passed away nearly 300 miles away in a locked building for the criminally insane.

I thought Sophie and I both grew up as God's motherless orphans. But at least she had a Father...... Maybe. .... And a Godsend in Miss Ellie.

LIST OF NEW FAMILY DOCUMENTS

- **Birth Certificate** – March 9, 1947 – **Sharline Ivy Sherman**. To Walters and Camille Sherman of DeLand, FL. There is no mention of a twin sister, but parts of the document are torn off, blank, marginally legible, and quite tattered.

- **Death Certificate** – February 23, 1951 – **Sharline Sherman.** Limited information due to the poor condition of the form. Fall downstairs. Nearly four years of age. (The same date of Camille's admission to the hospital and the "day the ambulance came").

- **Death Certificate** – June 2, 1952 – **Camille Maria Benoit Sherman.** Pneumonia. The mother of Sharline and Sophie Sherman. Estranged wife to Walters Sherman.

Documents that have been challenging to find

- **The birth certificate** was NOT found for **Sophie Sherman.** The probable date of birth and location are the same as Sharline's: March 9, 1947.

- **Police and Ambulance** records regarding "the day the ambulance came" on February 23, 1951, are NOT found.

Convinced there was little else I could find within public records, I turned my attention back to my primary task – reading the life and times of my Mother.

ONCE UPON MISPLACED TIME – 1957

As New Year's Eve sailed off and left 1957 anchored to the shore, I decided to include some news and events to better understand the times in which my Mother lived.

1957 brought with it an exciting variety of things.

- Frisbee came out from Wham-O

- Asian Flu kills about 70,000 people in the USA.

- *"American Bandstand"* makes its TV debut in August with Dick Clark

- *The Cat in the Hat* book came out by Dr. Suess

- Soviets test the H Bomb

Sophie was gaining comfort both within her writing and within herself. It was interesting to notice and read as she grew. In the meantime, the news of the world was accelerating. The space race emerged as the Russians launched Sputnik on October 4th. Elvis dominated the airwaves with "All Shook Up," *"Atlas Shrugged"* by Ayn Rand was published, and "Gunsmoke" was popular on television.

Sophie – Tuesday, Welcome to January 1, 1957. Happy New Year! I wonder what will happen this year. This is also the year I turn ten years old – double digits! My favorite TV show is Lassie. I wish I had a dog like that. Sophie

Sophie *– Friday, Jan 4, 1957. It is Randal's birthday. He is 16 years old – or something like 112 (I think) in dog years! Miss Ellie says she will help me make some chocolate chip cookies for him today as a present. She is so great. Sof*

Sophie *–Saturday, Jan 5, 1957. Randal thanked me for the cookies (Miss Ellie deserves the most credit here). He will look at and visit some colleges soon and wants to be a veterinarian. She took me for a haircut, and despite the "coolish" weather, I went into McCrory's and bought two malts to take out: chocolate banana for me and strawberry for her, with extra whipped cream. It is never too cold for malts! Sophie*

Sophie *- Sunday, January 6, 1957. Back to school tomorrow already. I can ride my new bike to school! I got a lock for it. Me*

Sophie *-Tuesday, February 4, 1957. I still remember when Miss Ellie showed me my "best friend" in the mirror when I was very young - maybe 4 or 5 years of age. She told me I could share all my hopes and dreams with her. How does she know? Miss Ellie says all girls dream and wish to be happy and beautiful. And all girls need a special friend to share secrets with. S*

Cindy – Sophie wrote about all kinds of personal things in her life – such as pies she made with Miss Ellie, shoes, shopping, clothes, toys, television, Mrs.

Williston's beloved dog, Cardinals, and Robins in the yard, and compost pile she was making for her gardens, friends. Sue's dog comes to the school playground every day. Billy has head lice. Dave brought his pet spider to class. Rose has a new baby sister and more. She was becoming more sociable – staying with friends and visiting other families with a daughter the same age and grade as Sophie.

Sophie – Saturday, March 9, 1957. Happy birthday to me, number 10! Miss Ellie made me some vanilla ice cream and red velvet cake (my favorite!). Nancy and Carol came over to spend the night. We set up a tent made of sheets and used sleeping bags on the floor between the twin beds in my room upstairs. Nancy brought a flashlight. Miss Ellie made some jiffy pop and Coke drinks. father asked me what the "ruckus" was all about. I told him it was a sleepover for my birthday. She gave me a birthday card from him with 3 dollars in it. Randal says he will take me for a malt at McCrory's for my birthday tomorrow! Sophie

Sophie – March 16, 1957. The scent of the azaleas woke me this morning from outside my bedroom window as the sun awakened the day from the east. Pink sunbeams reach to touch the sky gently. Then, a soft breeze awakes nature, and all is light and right in the world.

Sophie – Monday, March 18, 1957 – I told the mirror this morning – see, I still take very good care of her, and I showed her my Sophie rag doll. We both smiled.

SS

Sophie – Saturday, April 14, 1957 – We went shopping at Dreka's today to buy a dress for the Easter Sunday service. I found a light blue one that looks like a princess dress but is only shorter. Miss Ellie said it was her favorite color, and I looked like a princess. We had some money left over – so I asked the saleslady if I could look at some girl hats. She returned a beautiful straw hat with white satin daisy flowers to the dressing room. I asked Miss Ellie if she liked it. (I thought it was something Mrs. Williston would wear to church.) She said it was the prettiest hat she'd ever seen. I asked Miss Ellie to see what other girl hats they had and bring back one or two to the dressing room. While she was gone, I asked the saleslady if the daisy hat was available in a lady size. She said Yes. I told her we would buy it with this blue dress – but please put the lady hat in a bag so Miss Ellie would not see it. Then, Miss Ellie returned with two more hats for me to try on. I looked at them and said I think the daisy hat will work fine. So, we secretly bought the lady-size daisy hat and the dress for me. It was fun! Not that I like lying to Miss Ellie – but I think God will understand.

Dreka's Department Store, 1930s
N029957 DeLand, Florida
https://www.floridamemory.com/items/show/139539

Sophie – Saturday, April 20, 1957. As usual, Miss Ellie cleaned up the house and fixed breakfast. I asked her to sit at the dining room table and close her eyes. I put the pretty straw hat on her head and a hand mirror before her. I told her to open her eyes. She said, "What is this? I don't need no Easter bonnet!"

I said, "Well, now that you have one, you might as well wear it." Tears were in her eyes. I said, please don't cry. I wanted this to make you happy. She put me on her lap. She hugged me like I do my rag doll. Neither of us wanted to let go. Soph

Cindy – Dreka's was rebuilt in 1909 after a fire. It was the first building in the county built using concrete and remains in place today. The fire was quite an issue for wood buildings at the time. A massive fire along Woodland Boulevard on September 27, 1886, destroyed many businesses. Today, they are replaced with brick buildings containing the active and varied businesses along the Boulevard.

Sophie - Tuesday, April 30, 1957– Spring is my favorite time – many different butterflies are in my garden of sunflowers and wildflowers. Everything is beautiful in spring. Sophie

Sophie – Sunday, May 5, 1957 - Nature creates communities of love and sunshine. Nature welcomes sun and rain. It is shameless beauty for all. Harmony and love prevail, not hate; joy, not jealousy; community instead of communism. A garden grows hope – and love. Sophie

Sophie – Wednesday, May 8, 1957 – Miss Ellie tells me my favorite friend is in the mirror, and I must take good care of her. I dream of her– waiting for me. We are best friends...we are each other and share secrets.

Sophie - Saturday, May 18, 1957 – Miss Ellie would say that how you think of the world will change what you see in it. If you believe a person is evil, your brain will convince you that it is true - and that good-thinking people see good things and thoughts. Leeann won the spelling bee today when she spelled out chrysanthemum. I had to use my dictionary to get this right!! S

Cindy – I noticed she was no longer consistently adding her name to the end of each entry. Sometimes, she wrote "S" or "SS" or nothing at all. And there were also times when her writing approached snippets of poetic imagery and thought.

Sophie – *Monday, May 20, 1957 - Spring is like a flower garden – reborn from the heartless winter. School is out soon for the summer! I have a summer book reading list!*

Sophie - *Saturday, June 8, 1957 – Summer! June afternoon summer storms and the watermelon this year will be fantastic. 4th of July fireworks and the mosquitoes having a feast are coming soon! Randal's dog, Max, will again chase the fireflies once the sun goes down. Last year, the booms of the firecrackers scared Max, and he hid under the picnic table – so I sat down there with him and held him, and we watched the fireworks together. SS*

Sophie – *Tuesday, June 18, 1957 - We went to some very cold but refreshing Springs. I suppose sometimes, like this, it is a shame I can't swim. I have never even had a swimsuit.*

The Springs are just a few miles southwest and near the St John's River. Once we arrived, Miss Ellie took me to meet the beautiful lady in the water. I got down on my knees beside the water. There she was – alive in the clear water and shimmers of light dancing around the face of someone so happy to see me looking back. I reached out to touch her. At the same time, she reached out to touch me, and ripples sent shivers and sparkles through us both simultaneously. I felt a warmth in the cool water. I saw her patience, perseverance, and love. And big fishes swimming around her! "You were always the brave and forgiving one," I whispered to her.

"There you are. Two beautiful young ladies," Miss Ellie said quietly from behind.

Miss Ellie says life becomes meaningless without someone to care for. I care for my reflection. We share secrets between just us.

It is such days in places when I wonder if God ever gets lonely or jealous and longs to frolic among butterflies and trees on carefree days of contentment – maybe this is the place where God takes some time off. Sophie

Cindy – I can only guess this drawing came about as a tree she saw that day. Blue Spring State Park and its 72-degree clear water are a Florida State Park near present-day Orange City. It has the largest spring on the St John's River. It is well known as the place to see the manatees that visit each winter. It is also great for canoeing, swimming, hiking, scuba diving, and camping.

And Sophie was imaginative too! She created a character of her alter ego. Sierra Sommers shows up here and periodically throughout her diary.

Sophie – Tuesday, June 25, 1957. My secret hero – Sierra Sommers, is an only and very adventurous child. As a teenager, she wants to learn how to fly a plane, scuba dive, sail a boat to islands off Florida, and ride a horse to African villages to teach kids how to read and play games. And she likes to write!

Sophie – Thursday, July 4, 1957. It just is not the same without Randal and his guitar this year. Miss Ellie and I sat outside eating watermelon and drinking lemonade while watching the fireworks from the front porch. I didn't even want to see the parade this year. Poor Max stayed under Randal's bed. S

Sophie – Monday, August 12, 1957. School starts again soon. I will be in 5th grade. Funny, I remember when Miss Ellie first took me to kindergarten, and the school office lady asked for information. Miss Ellie turned to me and asked what my middle name was. I *said my name is Sophie Sherman. I had no idea what a middle name was. I still don't know if I ever had one. I asked father that night, and he said, "Why do you worry about that rot?" The office lady said I was too young to start kindergarten then, but Miss Ellie told her that Mr. Walters Sherman said it would be all right for me to start now. I started school the next day. Sophie*

Sophie *– Saturday, September 14, 1957. Nancy and I walked to the downtown area on the Boulevard and got a malt with her mother, Mrs. Northwell. We talked about school and the homework due next week, and Nancy told me secretly she likes that new boy, Dan. me*

Sophie *-Tuesday, September 17, 1957. Sierra Sommers's journeys are full of adventure and replace princess fairy tales with a healthy dose of reality. She saves plants from drought and pestilence. Her parents are British. Her Dad is a professor of English literature and poetry. Her Mom is a Botanist at a horticulture lab. Sierra is a bit artsy and loves science. "Life is not a destination - it is the journey." S*

Cindy – Sierra Sommers is an imaginary hero who entered the soul of its creator and took on life. In school, Sophie mentioned quite a bit about what she was learning about nature and integrated some of it into stories about Sierra.

She only wrote about her grades when she did not do as well as she wanted - "I got a blasted B+ on the

Florida History test." She would mention that her teachers said she was an excellent student on her report cards and how Miss Ellie would sign Walter's name on the report card so Sophie could return it to school as required.

Sophie also applied what she was learning about geography and humanity to her ongoing stories about Sierra Sommers...

Sophie – *Friday, October 18, 1957. Today, we find Sierra snorkeling in the Caribbean to collect conch and make fried breadfruit for her new friends. She had just returned from her trip to Africa, where she gave toys and picture books to the kids and brought rice and walnuts for the adults. Her goal is never to stop feeding the wonder of life. SS*

Cindy – Despite her young years, her writing and maturity progressed quickly.

Sophie - *Sunday, October 20, 1957. Sierra is a friend to animals and plants gardens of hope. She lives where she builds her dreams and needs no one to take care of her. She saves villages and plays with the children – her initials are the same as ours. She calls herself Sierra. She has room enough for all the hope, imagination, and ambition of three people. She thinks there is an art to allowing life to take you where you want to go.*

She also plays piano and harmonica when a piano is not nearby. She cooks pancakes on a campfire.

Sierra does not live life – life lives within her... And dreams to embrace before I sleep. She is a crusader for plants, animals, and people and does the work of two women – or, as Miss Ellie might say, 30 men. SS

Sophie - *Sleep, that strange, disjointed place of dreams where you don't question the muddled madness of life ... or the reality of your delusions.*

Cindy - Jonathan came by my house and asked how things were going. I asked him who Nancy was, as Sophie mentioned in the diary. He seemed to recall that she was a good friend in her class who lived nearby. What can you tell me about her Sierra Sommers stories? He knew nothing of her, but then, Sophie had a great imagination – with a serious, realistic streak.

Sophie – *Monday, November 4, 1957. I dream of another secret soulmate, of hopes and wishes, a friend — our ever-present secret companion – Sierra Sommers. Today, Sierra makes tea of thyme, cactus palm, and figs. And the children taught her to make baskets of leaves and vines.*

Sophie – *Friday, November 15, 1957. Novembers are a miserable excuse for a month – plants are dying, and short days suddenly become black nights as if a blanket is thrown over the town and choke the stars. Thanks for Thanksgiving and for forcing us to consider being grateful for something during this depressing time of year. SS*

***Sophie** - Thursday, November 21, 1957. Thanksgiving – going to Miss Ellies for dinner. Her Family shares clothes, recipes, stories, home, and lives. I am so jealous of Miss Ellie. Her home is small and tidy with functional comfort, hand-drawn pictures, framed photos on the walls of the family, and very few inherited items collecting dust or space for the extra clutter of more than what you need. You can close your eyes, listen, and feel the love in this place and people. They smile and hug each other. I will save some of my meal to take home to father. S*

***Sophie** – Tuesday, December 3, 1957. father attends commission meetings in the evenings, sleeps most of the day during weekends, goes on business trips and bank meetings, and goes into his office. He used sometimes to read me fairy tales of adventure with charming castles in faraway lands, beautiful white horses, and princes, and then there were the angry times with me huddled behind closed closet doors, careful not to make any sound. I played Jingle Bells and Silent Night on the school piano at the Christmas program for the parents. Miss Ellie gave me some flowers afterward. SS*

***Sophie** – Thursday, December 5, 1957. Sierra has a camera and takes pictures of wildlife, children, and exotic plants worldwide. Next, she wants to fly a two-seat plane to the Galapagos to see the giant turtles.*

Randal likes animals – I wonder what he would think of giant turtles. Sophie

Cindy – Sophie sometimes writes ideas about Sierra Sommers and her thoughts and adventures. Such as *Sierra uniting all life into an endless quest to explore.* And seemingly random snippets of ideas and parts of sentences or thoughts ... *Maybe Sierra can reunite families across time... The soul refreshes itself with a quiet morning awakening and becomes comfortable with the authentic self.*

It is quite creative at times. And despite her young years, Sophie was growing up quickly, and, at times, I questioned if she was attempting to escape some underlying depression. She also insists on writing "father" with a lowercase f.

She also mentions people in her school. Miss Henries got into a hornet nest, and one eye was swollen. Sue's dog comes to the school playground each day to play catch. Dave brought his pet spider to class. John had a cigarette in his pocket.

Sophie – *Saturday, December 7, 1957. I hate the stupid clock on the fireplace mantle downstairs. The clock lost its gentle chime years ago. It can only make the endless annoying noise of "now" ... "now" ... "now" ... For 60 times each minute, it buries the present into an ever-growing pile of "now" history and continuously deprives the future of more time. Instead, I would like it to sound like – "I hate it." "I hate it." "I hate it." Maybe then that hateful, ugly clock would die of self-inflicted abuse. And I can hear it up here in my room – even with the door closed and a blanket stuffed under it. It* *reminds me how this eternity of now is slowly sliding off the mantel and hitting the floor bit by bit.*

How do you live in the NOW – or rather, how do you not live in the now? You prepare for the future – yet when you arrive there (if possible), it is the now. In school, we are taught to change our future – what about working on improving our NOW? So many people need help – now. Sophie

Sophie *– Wednesday, December 11, 1957. Money appears to be the creator of all things, dazzling and wrong. It causes hope and hopelessness. I learned from overhearing father yelling at some poor man from the bank on the phone. Money determines everything, even when some things are more important – how much cash decides what happens and what does not. S*

Cindy - Sophie also writes about doppelganger plants and how lookalikes can be a trap and a means to protect the plant. *There are "evil twins" among plants and insects that trick you. They can make you sick – or "just dead."* And she added, perhaps as an afterthought – *"I can't help but notice how so many pet dogs resemble their owner too, like Sinatra with Mrs. Williston. And Max with Randal. I wonder what my pet would look like – if I had one. I want a small one that is endlessly happy! Soph"*

Sophie- *Tuesday, December 24, 1957. Last year, I saw Miss Ellie wrapping gifts that I later found under* *the Christmas tree with labels from Santa. I also saw her bring in a bag from her car with presents. Santa is just another "make believe" – like castles and a prince to rescue you and take you off to happily ever after. Is hope just a pathetic joke? Even the Christmas tree looks sad this year. S*

Cindy – I am worried about Sophie.

REFLECTED SILENCE – 1958

Events in 1958 include:

- *Witch Doctor* by David Seville is the same guy who does the Chipmunks.

- Presbyterian Church Cornerstone was set on November 30, 1958, at 724 North Woodland Blvd.

- The Hula Hoop is popular.

- Slinky Dogs, Mr. Potato Head, Playdoh, Matchbox cars, Yo-yos, and Pogo sticks.

- The US Congress created the National Aeronautics and Space Administration (NASA) on July 29th.

- The *Purple People Eater* song by Sheb Wooley.

Sophie – Wednesday, January 1, 1958. OK – A New Year should start on a new day at the start of a new week. Starting on a Wednesday of a half-used-up, leftover week from last year does not feel right. It tarnishes the entire excitement and hope of the all-new and better. Still the same ole me, though - Sophie

Sophie – Saturday, January 4, 1958. Randal birthday number 17. He finishes high school this year. He was able to take advanced classes and will start college soon. He is an intelligent guy. Sophie

Sophie – Monday, January 6, 1958. A layer of brutal cold settled atop everything and rudely assaulted my bare feet on the floor first thing this morning. Gray clouds hung where the barren trees poked and bruised the sky. I still and will always hate January.

Sophie – Wednesday, February 12, 1958. I had to walk to Woolworths to buy some stupid candy and stuff for Valentine's Day. Nancy went with me. She has the same thoughts as me – I rather have the day off school to get my garden ready for planting soon. If Valentine's Day could be on Saturday, we could have some home parties, and maybe since that would make Friday the 13, we could all write papers about unlucky things that have happened to each of us. I guess it just feels good to complain today. But – Nancy and I did get to eat some of the candy on the way home and bought a malt. That made it worth it, and it was good to talk with Nancy.

Sophie – Friday, Feb 14, 1958. Valentine's Day is on Friday, so Saturday would be better. I don't understand the card and candy thing. Miss Ellie says someday I will. Right now, it just gets in the way, and I am not sure what to do with all the cards that have no meaning and cheap candy – so just like the clothes, toys, and books I outgrow, I let Miss Ellie find homes for it all. I am guessing she throws out the cards. S

Sophie – Sunday, March 9, 1958. – Happy birthday

to me - number 11! I saved up part of my allowance over the past year and bought myself a camera and some film for my birthday! It is a beautiful 35mm Canon camera and some Kodak film. I will be reading the instructions for quite a while, but I can't wait to take pictures! I told Miss Ellie that Nancy, I, and maybe Carol and Pam would get food downtown for my birthday. I didn't need any dinner. SS

Sophie *- Wednesday, March 19, 1958. – We looked at some microscopes today in science class. The teacher brought some water from the river – under the microscope. It was terrific! Critters were moving all around! How can you look up at the stars above or peer into teaming life under a microscope and not believe in a master genius somewhere? There is so much more than we can see or understand. Sophie*

Sophie *– Thursday, April 10, 1958. Randal is graduating high school soon. He wants to go to be a veterinarian. He is six or so years older than me. He will be gone for years, except for some short breaks here and there. What will I do without him to answer my questions and keep me looking forward beyond what tomorrow brings? S*

Cindy – I keep reminding myself that Randal to her is the aging Jonathan Peterson to me. I try to envision them both young and anxious for what lies ahead. Sophie's diary posts were becoming more social as she wrote about school clubs, teachers, school events, local events, dancing, piano recitals, television, music on the radio, the Athens Theater, and traffic on the road.

Sophie – Saturday, April 26, 1958. Miss Ellie told me how a friend's child was made fun of in a nearby park for being Negro. She was sitting in the sandbox and crying before her mother could chase off the tormentors and rescue her. Other children had kicked sand at her and called her names. One boy peed on her right there in the sandbox. And their parents did nothing.

Maybe we are animals, after all. I asked Miss Ellie if this ever happened to her – how does she handle such rudeness? She said, "I hold my head high, keep my eyes forward, and walk toward a brighter day. I try to forgive ignorance. But it is not an easy thing to do. You must be brave and strong."

I am not sure I could do that.

Sophie – Thursday, May 1, 1958. Miss Ellie says people like to think happiness is just around the corner. She said planning for your future is wonderful, but don't forget that joy only lives in the NOW. She also said, "When it comes to planning, nature and time are always several steps ahead of you. Planning is a great thing to do, Miss Sophie, but accept it seldom exactly matches what happens."

Sophie – Thursday, May 8, 1958. Miss Ellie says that sometimes, everyone realizes that NOW is all we have. How do we make the best of it? NOW is where we live and where we die. Improving the future and changing the world are determined by what we are doing NOW. She is so smart, brave, and truthful about things. Sophie

Sophie *– Thursday, May 15, 1958. I asked Randal what it feels like to be graduating soon. He said he is partly happy, excited, and scared. Moving away to go to college is going to change everything for him. And college is HARD – but he is willing and mostly ready to do it. Going to John B. Stetson University nearby would be much easier, but they do not offer the degree he wants.*

Cindy – Sophie wrote about her butterfly (mostly Monarch and Swallowtail), dragonfly, and firefly collections. She took pictures with her new camera, practiced classical music, did some piano recitals, and wrote snippets of poetry. Randal's dad, Dr. Peterson, took her horseback riding a few times at a nearby ranch, which she immensely enjoyed. There were movies with school friends, shopping with Miss Ellie, record playing, and dances. Her posts were becoming both more introspective and included more social encounters.

Sophie - *Friday, June 6, 1958. School is out today! It is already hot outside. I am looking for a babysitting job to get me away from home more. I want to spend more time at Miss Ellie's place. I want a family like hers. They share clothes, food, stories, homes, and lives. They understand each other well enough to guess their* *needs without words. They love each other.*

I remember Miss Ellie used to read bedtime stories to me. Her words took me into another world. Once I knew all the stories by heart, she would open the book and pretend to read it aloud as she created a new fairy tale. Suddenly, lollipops grew on trees, and Princess Sophie had the magic to push away mosquitoes during the Fourth of July fireworks. Birds sang the happiest songs while sliding down a rainbow and into the garden. The kingdom was filled with gentle people, and happiness fell from the heaven above. She made my world into one far away and happy.

Cindy - And after previously being worried about her being depressed, optimism started showing up often in her writings.

Sophie *– Saturday, June 7, 1958. It felt good to sleep late today. I stayed there and enjoyed the comfy bed and birds singing outside my window. I thought about how Miss Ellie says church tells you how to be a good person. But even if you don't attend church, you can still do something good for another person daily. You can pay notice to the good that surrounds us all the time. Just noticing the good everywhere will make you feel happier and be a better person. Maybe that happened to father – he could not see the good. Soph*

Sophie *- Wednesday, June 11, 1958. I went to the John B. Stetson University Sampson Library to learn more about plants I can grow in the backyard. There* *are encyclopedias there. I can see pictures of plants there, and the librarian is very helpful. I planted flowers and had a vegetable garden in the yard. Green peppers are doing well – but the tomatoes have some bugs. There is shameless beauty in the dirt. No jealousy, no commies (Mrs. Williston says that) under every bed. A garden grows only hope. I took pictures of the veggies I grew!*

Cindy – The Sampson Library opened in 1908 within the John B. Stetson University campus. It was named after university trustee C.T. Sampson, a significant donor to the library fund who bequeathed $20,000 to the library.

And then, some entries could do with insight into what inspired or promoted it.

Sophie *– Friday, June 13, 1958. I sometimes question whether reality is actual or just something for us struggling to believe in something to give us hope. I wonder what reality for father is like. I need to work in the front garden today. Happy Friday, the 13th!*

Sophie *– Sunday, June 15, 1958. Went to church again today with Mrs. Williston.*

She says that when you are young, everything is given to you – clothes, food, a roof, time, courage, encouragement, and hope. It is all taken from you in old age - in pieces at a time. You must find joy waiting for you in the tiny bits left. Then she said, - have we not learned enough yet? In war, there are no winners. It is much like old age – the loss, the pain. You are left with only memories – if you are fortunate. Old age quietly lures you into its trap and takes hostages daily in small, measured doses. Your friends and pets pass away. Eyesight diminishes, and memories fade. Some of my acquaintances still waste time grooming their vanity. I get more joy from covering the mirrors in my home.

I think she is just lonely. I hope to grow old with graceful acceptance and gratitude.

Cindy – And then Sophie sometimes showed her somewhat mystic side.

Sophie – *Wednesday, June 18, 1958. Maybe visiting angels are just soul mates reflected in various places and shadows on the ground. They provide hope that we will meet again along paths in quiet places without gravity or the confines of time.*

Cindy - Sophie was quite upset when her father, in a drunken rage or perhaps stupor, drove his Studebaker through her garden of sunflowers and wildflowers. The next day, Randal helped replant and arrange the bricks and stones to protect them from Walters's indiscretion and misdirection through life. She writes:

"*Murdered plants everywhere - by a Studebaker*"

Sophie – *Friday, June 20, 1958. father ran his car over all the flowers I had planted and tended to in the* *front yard. I was mad because he hurt my feelings. I was angry that he did not seem to care. I was mad because I wondered if it was intentional, and I was mad if it was carelessness. I was angry that he did not apologize. I was upset because he hurt the plants - they are my friends. I wonder (or not) how he would react if I were to do the same damage to his "friendly" bottle. If God is all-powerful, wise, and great, why does he create such people? I dreamed last night that vibrant, beautiful wildflowers had grown all over and above the house and into the heavens – but later, they became dry, brittle weeds that poked holes into the sunlight and stars above with their thorns. It appeared to be the death of my summer.*

Cindy – Thankfully, her attitude changed a bit the next day as she wrote –

Sophie *– Saturday, June 21, 1958. Thankfully, Randal, being the great person he is, helped me to fix the garden father plowed with his car. We put up some bricks and stones to hopefully protect the plants and provide some noisy warning should father decide on performing Act II. Thankfully, father parked in the driveway today instead of the flowerbed. Somehow, I think he expects a standing ovation.*

Sophie *– Thursday, June 24, 1958. Randal is going away today to see a college he wants to attend. What will we do without him around? I miss him so much already. I admire him so much. He asked me if I would play with Max now and then and take him for walks.*

How wonderful is that! I love Max! He is such a great dog! That makes it a little bit easier when Randal is gone. Randal is my Prince Charming – for real.

***Sophie** – Thursday, June 26, 1958. I was so upset with my father, and I was avoided by others, afraid to talk with me when walking Max, when at church, or with my friends. I guess everyone has heard about how he managed to miss the driveway in front of the house entirely the other day- in view of all neighbors, God, and the entire universe – to plant his car into my garden. Miss Ellie said - No one gets through this life without getting upset, being a bit damaged, and carrying some heavy baggage. The trick is finding peace with it, accepting it, and keeping going anyway. That part of NOW is over. Live your current Now like it is brand new – because it is.*

Cindy – Then there were entries with little explanation to set the stage.

***Sophie** – Tuesday, July 1, 1958. Miss Ellie said, "We are not far enough from history yet for white folk to like us, and I fear an uprising that some are talking of will make that worse. Some Colored folks hate White people, too. We must find a way to trust each other because we all want the same thing. People must be intolerant of the intolerance that makes no matter. When life puts holes in your soul, you must refill them with love and patience."*

<u>Before I forget, I want to write down some things</u>

<u>Miss Ellie says because the lady is brilliant</u>.

- *Live love.*

- *Do not allow rage to eat your soul.*

- *Love what we have in common.*

- *Wisdom and kindness live in quiet places.*

Cindy – And then - some entries were submitted by Sierra as well....

Sierra - *Wednesday, July 9, 1958. God watches over the little children of the world. Today, African children taught me how to make special bread of wild figs. I took pictures of the children! Sierra*

Sophie - *Monday, July 21, 1958. Wonder changes you. When you're under the spell, all you see is hope. You and Mother Nature are connected to all life, past, present, and future. It is a lovely place without pain. I must get back there. SS*

Cindy – I wondered if the signature of "SS" at the end of her entry was for Sophie Sherman, Sierra Sommers, Sophie & Sierra, or Sophie and Sharline. She not only wrote with insight and talked about the nature of plants and animals but also drew darn well. Here and there in the diary were hand-drawn pictures. This flower had no explanation. It was just there - on the paper.

Sophie - *Friday, August 1, 1958. Carol is moving to Ohio. Her Father has a new job. They are leaving before school starts. I both will miss her and envy her. The science and art conference will be at John B. Stetson this weekend. I have friends to catch up with there.*

Sophie – *Sunday, August 17, 1958. Randal went off to go back to college after a quick visit again today. My best buddy and dear friend are gone. Aloneness is everywhere. Nothing fills the space that he so filled up with his presence. I promised to walk Max every day and provide plenty of TLC. Max is a great dog. He is always glad to see me. I plan to bathe him this weekend or try to get him wetter than me. We will see how that goes! I need to work this out.*

***Sophie** – Friday, August 29, 1958. After some friends spent the night last night, father said, "No more friends here. They are noisy and too pretty!" What does that mean, Miss Ellie – why would he say this? I don't understand. I like my friends. We stay upstairs in my room – we don't bother him. Why is he so mean? Miss Ellie says it means you spend the night at their homes instead of here when you want to spend time with your friends.*

Becky told me her Father took her to a special daughter/Father dinner and bought her roses for her birthday. Donna said Mr. Jacobs took a picture of his oldest daughter in her prom dress and had a local artist paint her portrait from it to hang in the living room. Mr. Tyler taught his daughter how to drive and shoot a gun and took her and his son on hunting trips. What am I doing wrong? What must I do to get a compliment, thanks, or a kind word from my father?

***Sophie** – Wednesday, September 17, 1958. I noticed a long-forgotten book on my bookcase: Cinderella. Lately, I have seen the quick passing of time, and I feel compelled to write about my childhood before more memory passes. Miss Ellie read this book to me most evenings when I was young. It was about a neglected, overlooked girl who was rescued by and married a prince and lived happily ever after. I grew up thinking that is what happens to everyone in everyday life. Prince Charming is out there and looking for me. But perhaps the truth is that I am a temporary hitchhiker on a runaway train about to tumble off a cliff in the* middle of nowhere and surrounded by nothing in all directions.

Sophie - *Saturday, October 18, 1958. Last night, a ruckus and "thump" was followed by a moan. Before I could get to my bedroom door, Miss Ellie was there. She was out of breath from running up the stairs.*

"Your father fell. He is drunk. He hit his head, but he was all right. Please lock your door and go back to sleep," she said.

In the morning, father was asleep sitting up in the armchair downstairs. He had dried blood on his face and arms. His clothing was not fastened. I called the doctor to come and see him. Dr. Wilson came to the house by 10 a.m. I told him that my father had fallen last night.

To that, father said, "No, I did not!" He said, "That Negro Nanny of yours hit me with that sterling platter over there."

Doctor Wilson provided a sideways glance and asked, "Why would Miss Ellie hit you?"

"You need to ask her that," father said.

Doc examined the wound on his head. He cleaned away the old blood and put a dressing over a big bump on his left forehead. Doctor Wilson told father to rest today and put cold compresses on his head. And no whiskey for two days. Doc told me to call him if father got confused or would not wake up.

***Sophie** – Monday, October 20, 1958. I stayed home from school today to stay with my father. I am missing some significant exams and will have to find some story and means to find a way to get excused and be allowed to take the exams.*

Miss Ellie came here just before noon time. I told Miss Ellie what Doctor Wilson and father said about the platter. She said – "Child, you have good reason not to trust your father at times.... And yes, I did hit him with that platter."

I said, "I am sure he deserved it."

Miss Ellie came up with good advice. She said, "Let's leave history in its time. He got the message. Nuf said. Wisdom is knowing when the rules won't work."

It was still too tempting for her to keep completely quiet. "Often, men folks have created a world for themselves – and often they deserve it! Miss Sophie, if you ever need me, all you need to do is call. You are very precious to me. I thank God for you each night, and I wish you were my daughter. I will bring you to my house, and you can stay there."

How am I going to explain my absence to the school? I can't let anyone know about father. What would Randal do? The secrets I keep from the world are building a cave around me.

Miss Ellie brought a rope ladder to escape out the front window of my bedroom if I ever needed to get out of the house. We rolled it up and put it near my bedroom window upstairs. She told me to lock my bedroom door every night and not to let my father in if he had been drinking. Then she said she was no longer staying the night. Instead, she would arrive early in the morning to ensure I had what I needed to get off, prepare for school, and do some laundry. Then, she would return at about 4 p.m. to prepare dinner and catch up with what I was doing at school and other things before going home.

Miss Ellie has lived in our home since I was almost four years old. Usually, she would also spend the night – but less so as the years passed. Before I started school, she took me everywhere with her. We met her family, friends, her group of church ladies, and more. As time passed, she mainly stayed only during the day, fixed meals, cleaned, and took me grocery shopping, where we bought some hamburgers wrapped in new stuff called cellophane! She took me to a school play practice, music lessons, doctor appointments, and special outings. She is exceptional. She is gentle and kind and very wise beyond all measure.

Miss Ellie has an old car she drives – not sure what kind it is, but it rattles. We also walk a lot to stores and places too. I am very proud of her and hope she is proud of me. She is my mother and my friend.

Sophie – *Tuesday, October 21, 1958. I went back to school today. No one asked me about not being here yesterday. I can only guess they are afraid to ask or do not care. Not sure which is worse.*

Sophie – *It is Halloween! I remember, long ago, a porcelain doll was on a shelf in our bedroom. She had a pink dress, blond hair, and big dark eyes. At night, when color faded, her eyes, dress, and pale skin became ghost-like. I screamed! Miss Ellie climbed up a ladder and took the doll away – forever.*

Sophie – *Thursday, November 18, 1958. This evening, I packed toys, clothes, and things for Miss Ellie to give to children and others who would like them. This week, I am helping her make cookies and food for the church folk she knows. I asked her if she knew someone who could use the big crib in the attic – and she smiled. "The church could use it in the childcare area while the parents are in church," she replied. "We would be most grateful, but I suppose you should check with your father to make sure it is all right to do that."*

I thought father does not /cannot get up to the attic, nor would he know what to do with the oversized crib – if indeed he remembers it. But then - I almost forgot, I cannot talk about what everyone has known for all my 11 years. Besides, I had just grown to assume the extra bed in my bedroom was for Miss Ellie and my friends, but I also knew that was not the original intent.

"Miss Ellie," I said, "Let's find a way to make it happen to get that crib to your church. If I recall correctly, you took it apart when you dragged it upstairs years ago. I will get it downstairs, out the back porch door, and clean it up. You might need to take a few trips to get all the parts into your car. But we can do this. Please – my only request is that you don't tell anyone whom it came from. I don't want to talk about it to anyone. Please. Deal?"

Miss Ellie looked at me, silently nodded, and hugged me.

__Sophie__ – Thursday, November 27, 1958. Miss Ellie provided us with some Thanksgiving food and a pumpkin pie. I warmed them up for dinner and set the table for father and me. He ate everything I put on his plate. When I asked if it was good, he said yes. He turned on the TV, sat on the sofa, and slept. I washed up the dishes and put the leftovers in the refrigerator. I read a book about how to make your compost for gardens. Hardly an exciting evening.

__Sophie__ – Monday, December 8, 1958. According to Miss Ellie, there are those with whom you only share this time in this place. And then there are those not here or may have gone on, yet you still meld into perfect harmony. You know what they think, how they feel, and what makes us each happy. For Miss Ellie, that person is her long-deceased daughter. For me – she is within my vanity mirror.

I recall when I was very young, Miss Ellie and I would snuggle under the blankets at night to keep warm and have happy dreams. Together, we quietly made the world go away and shared comfort and safety. There, I became the essence of her daughter, and she became my sister.

Sophie – *Friday, December 12, 1958, evening – I put up a small Christmas tree I bought from a street vendor. He delivered it in his small truck and helped me to get the stand on it to set it up straight. I got the tree decorations from the far closet and arranged the manger scene by the fireplace. There is choir practice tonight for our performance at Sunday service. The Pastor's wife has the robe ready for me.*

Sophie – *Monday, December 15, 1958. Randal came home to be with his family over Christmas. I asked for some time so he could tell me about college and what it was like.*

Sophie – *Friday, December 19, 1958. Randal took me to McCrory's for a hamburger and malt and to buy a Christmas card. He told me about classes and lots of homework, and the friends he was making in class and playing soccer on Saturday nights. He was having a great time but working very hard. He missed Max and me a lot and wanted to hear about what I was doing and how school was going for me. I told him I liked just about everything in science – but felt like I was the only girl who did. He told me there is a young lady in his class who plans to be a veterinarian, too. Girls can do* *anything, and do not ever forget that! He also said he hoped to return to town in February because he wanted to see the race in Daytona on the new track, not the beach! I pretended like I had some clue about what he was talking about. Sophie*

Sophie *– Thursday, December 25, 1958. I saved up my allowance from Mr. O'Reilly (father's accountant) and bought Miss Ellie some warm slippers for her sore feet and some credit at the Winn Dixie store for whatever food she wanted. And I went to Stetson Flower shop and bought her a small vase of red roses. At first, I felt terrible when she cried – until she gave me the biggest hug anyone could ever hope for.*

I gave Randal two framed photographs I had taken of Max for him to take back to college. He was thrilled.

POST CARDS FROM GOD

1959 was the start of the end of a decade. As things got more complicated and moved faster, it happened closer to home. It brought with it:

- Two very different states join the United States of America – Hawaii, and Alaska

- A plane crash in Iowa kills Buddy Holly, Ritchie Valens, and J. P. Richardson (Big Bopper), along with the pilot.

- The Holiday House Restaurant opens at 704 N. Woodland Blvd in DeLand, Florida.

- Bobby Darin sings Mack the Knife

- News of unrest in Vietnam continues.

- A Tropical Storm hit DeLand on June 18 and another on October 19

- Twilight Zone started its programs on TV.

- Chatty Cathy dolls are for sale.

- The first Barbie Doll is displayed at the American Toy Fair in New York City. The original Barbie Doll was introduced on March 9, 1959.

Sophie - *Sunday, January 4, 1959. Randal turns 18*

today! Miss Ellie and I made a bunch of sugar and oatmeal cookies for him to take with him. He leaves in two days. I miss him already.

Sophie *– Saturday, January 17, 1959. I awoke this morning and helped Miss Ellie and some friends pick oranges off trees in Lake Helen today. There were so many of them! Several children came to help also. It was a lot of work, but I enjoyed it! Several children were chasing each other and throwing rotten oranges at each other. I helped pick and gather the good oranges and get them into the trucks. I am going to sleep very well tonight.*

Cindy - At the time, the central Florida area was miles of citrus trees, cows, and swamps along long, straight (and often dirt), two-lane roads.

Sophie *– February quietly snuck into the calendar last night but still with no sign of salvation. If there were ever a time when trees needed leaves, it would be in winter as some clothing to dull the cold everywhere.*

Sophie *– Thursday, February 19, 1959. While lying in bed this morning, I figured out how to fix my bicycle, use the tools, and adjust the chain, seat, and handlebars. I found father's tools in the garage. The bike is much easier to ride now. He never asks where I am going – but I try to tell him anyway. I think kids are supposed to do that. I leave Miss Ellie a note if I am somewhere other than school. I have to go to the running club tomorrow. Lately, I bring my gym shoes to* *school with me and run home from school – but that means I also must walk to school – because I don't want to leave my bike there at night. Gotta go! Ss*

Sophie *- Monday, March 9, 1959. Happy birthday, number 12! With our birthday money, I bought a film for the camera. After school, I also met friends at Tom's Pizza on East Rich Avenue. They put a candle on the pizza and sang Happy Birthday to us!*

*(**Sierra** jumps in here) - Barbie's (doll) official birthday is also March 9, 1959 —today, she was officially "born," I guess (as she is fully grown) and introduced to the world. I saw information on TV about Barbie Doll. I loved the idea of an "adult" doll that could grow up to do whatever job a girl could dream of - but I also hated princess clothes, fashion stuff, and high heels while wearing a swimsuit!!? It negated the idea of being your own person. I would support her right to do this. Still, I would rather see Barbie riding a horse, flying a plane, helping to build a church in South America, working in an orphanage or as a veterinarian, or dressed in a Girl Scout Leader uniform and cooking marshmallows at a campfire with young girls. Barbie could use a pair of leather boots and a hat that accommodates her ponytail. Already, McCall's is selling patterns for Barbie outfits that include wedding gowns, princess dresses, formal gowns, and more. I am not sure this is what I would do, but I am perhaps not a good judge of that! Sierra*

father gave us $20 this evening and then asked us

to buy him whiskey from Mr. Paul at the corner store. In the early evening, Miss Ellie took me to her house for a birthday cake and gave me an embroidery kit. We talked about all kinds of things. I love this woman. SS

Cindy – I was impressed by how quickly she changed personas between herself and Sierra. Perhaps that also contributed to her frequent use of the plural personal reference, such as we, us, and ours.

Sophie *– Saturday, March 14, 1959. According to Miss Ellie, all light and kindness are born in heaven. And just accepting that makes even the bad times better for all. Science does not seem to support the logical concept of heaven. Truthfully, Heaven sounds like it might get boring after a bit. S&S*

Sophie *– Tuesday, March 24, 1959. Who watches the world and keeps mistakes from ruining lives when God sleeps?*

Cindy – I am guessing that Sophie had a busy social life with friends this year, as her diary posts were less frequent and more eloquent.

Sophie *– Monday, April 13, 1959. I awoke this morning to catch the scent of nearby orange blossoms! It was delightful. I asked Miss Ellie, "How can you see the wildflowers determined to brighten up the barren soil in an otherwise ignored patch of land and not believe in the genius of God?" Miss Ellie said that it is like rainbows. It is a postcard from God - a moment or message where He lets you know he is thinking just of* *you. So many others walk by the very same thing and never notice because it is a beautiful gift of kindness specific to you at that moment. For example - Wildflowers grace cracks in sidewalks, flourish in playgrounds, and grow along the side of the road and beside trashcans. They bring joy to neglected places and make themselves at home anywhere with the intent to defeat the dullness. They are proof that Mother Nature is an artist.*

.... I just remembered that there is a Hoola Hoop competition today after class. Sandra told me she plans to win it!

Sophie *– Friday, May 22, 1959. Life and war can be such lonely places. Each person travels through life alone, simultaneously occupying a single space and time. Where do moment and site meet completely to intersect with that of others? I suppose bullets do just that- they rudely and abruptly invade the time and space of others at their opportune moment – with painful results. How can someone who knows nothing about another person – randomly kill them, and why?*

Cindy – I am unsure what news events of the time may have influenced this post – but likely related to events in Vietnam. The pain dug deeper into her soul.

Sophie *– (no date) Here are questions I want to ask Miss Ellie later ...if the spirit survives once a body dies, what is the point in having a body? It requires care, puts itself on a grand scale, demands attention, and creates* *pockets to fill with greed...what's the point of having a blasted body that makes a mess of everything? When does the joy of the moment surpass the despair of the future...*

Good cannot survive without evil. How could you appreciate good if it were not for the comparison with evil? Enough with the unanswerable madness.... Gotta go grab some yummies and walk Max.

Sophie** – Saturday, June 6, 1959. Miss Ellie says all people have "holes in their souls" somewhere. Everyone has something they are not proud of, something controlled by something (like whiskey) that they cannot always stop. Whatever it is, Miss Ellie is wise beyond her means. Her "holes" let the sunshine in and push out the bad. **So, how do you hide the ghost living in your soul?

Cindy – Ghost? I so wish at times I could talk with my young mother, Sophie!

***Sophie** – Monday, June 8, 1959. School is out for the summer. Randal should be home soon. Becky, from school, has become a good friend. Becky plays flute and wants to attend Stetson when she graduates high school and become a music teacher. So, we are thinking of finding a song where I can play piano, and she can play her flute. The challenge is finding a time when father is not home. And I have not practiced piano for a while because "the noise" bothers him.*

***Sophie** – Tuesday, June 16, 1959. My vegetable*

garden is doing well! I saw a rabbit today – but he did not do much damage. Some deer show up around here at times, too. But – I have some green beans and kale doing well. Miss Ellie is looking forward to cooking with them soon. The petunias in my front yard – and Mrs. Williston's are doing great. I need to water them all today as the afternoon thunderstorms have not started up reliably yet.

Sophie *– Friday, June 19, 1959. Wow! I mentioned we are awaiting afternoon thunderstorms on Tuesday, and yesterday, we got whopped with a big one! A big storm dumped LOTS of water, and many fallen, broken tree branches blocked the Boulevard. Crews are trying to clear city streets now. We lost power for a few hours.*

Sophie *-Tuesday, June 23, 1959. I spoke again to my best friend. I turned off the light on my vanity, hoping the light would linger longer before going dark. It hurts so to see her go. Sometimes, I leave on the light all night to ensure she is still there and doing OK. SS*

Cindy – She writes so well yet leaves many questions.

Sophie *– Saturday, July 4, 1959. We watched fireworks from Randal's front porch as they lit up the sky beyond the trees. His parents, Max, Miss Ellie, and I were there. We had watermelon, lemonade, and cookies (which Miss Ellie and I made earlier today). Randal told us how to make a grilled cheese sandwich with an iron and ironing board in his dorm room! Miss*

Ellie thought that was a great idea! A bit later, he got out his guitar. He played, and we sang "The Purple People Eater" and "Do You Want to Dance?" Miss Ellie and I could not stay still for that, and we tried not to hurt each other as we danced in the front yard behind some tall azaleas. Max chased the fireflies as they came out, and I tried to catch one gently to watch it flash in my hands. As always, Max did not like the big booms with fireworks, so I sat on the ground with him and held him in my lap. He was content there – but he still was not a big fan of the sudden noise. Max and I are great pals.

Sophie *– Friday, August 21, 1959. Already, Randal leaves today to go back to college again. He is doing so well, changing fast, and is concerned about all animals. He asked me about my father, and I told him things were the same. Max, his dog, was so happy to see Randal when he came home. He is sad when Randal goes away, so we go for walks daily, play, and chase after fireflies in the yard for fun in the evenings.*

Sophie *– Monday, September 14, 1959. Miss Ellie does not know when her birthday is – but probably sometime between 1900 and 1905. She was born at home in Georgia, and her mother died when she was young. I told Miss Ellie I wanted to take her to the Holiday House for her "whenever it is" birthday on Saturday, September 19th.*

She said, "Oh Lordy, Miss Sophie, they won't let me in the place! White folks seem to think that dark skin is contagious."

Not that I understand any of that mess – they allow criminals to eat there, people who cheat on their taxes, and Mr. Jones, who shot his neighbor's dog last year. Miss Ellie does none of that.

So, I planned a different surprise.

Sophie *- Saturday, September 19, 1959. A Back Porch Queen Lunch – I tied a scarf over Miss Ellie's eyes when she arrived at about 11 a.m. and gently led her to a table and chairs on the back porch. Awaiting her was a tiara and her lunch of pork roast with carrots and potatoes and the most enormous slice of their chocolate cake ever – with Iced tea using our best (and long neglected) glasses, silverware, and china. Tablecloth, folded linen napkins, and I bought some flowers for her on the table.*

I removed her scarf, and I curtsied and bowed. Miss Ellie was overwhelmed and claimed she felt like royalty – which was precisely the intent! Eventually, I got her to sit at the table and put a tiara on her head. (OK – it was made of foil wrap and rhinestones).

The air was just a hint of cool crisp. The early afternoon sun was kind and retreated gently behind the large tree. We ate with pinky finger extended and talked about the jewelry we had made and how the country club was such a delightful place at this time of year. I asked her what kind of car she fancied (a big bright red Cadillac) – and I asked, "Shall that be the new car you wish to drive to pick up the poodle from the groomers today?"

Whenever she tried to re-enter reality, I would do what I could to bring her back into the fairy tale. "Your Royal Highness, what shall be the cookies you would have with the afternoon tea today?" "Shall I shine those shoes up for you a bit?" Or – "I have prepared your gown for the ball tonight, and I am sure you will love it!" Upon finishing "the very best meal I have ever thought was possible," - I lit the candle on a slice of cake as tears welled in her eyes. As I sang happy birthday to her, I could see the grateful inner child longing to be a princess and surrounded by love. When you feel beloved, smiles come easily. In a box was the rest of the cake and meal to take home to her friends and "family."

Miss Ellie then took my hands, looked into my eyes, and said, "When my daughter passed, I cried till I thought I could never stop. The sorrow got deeper and deeper until it ate up my soul. She was my life and my happiness. She made me a better person. I never thought I could ever love another child as much until Miss Sophie, I met you. Thank you for giving me hope, making love from nothing, and giving it to so many."

Sophie *- Saturday, October 10, 1959. Of all the months, October is my absolute favorite! The slight coolness fills the days with tantalizing sounds, smells, and senses. It provides pumpkins and spices that I love*

– and is a bit of the comfy closing act before miserable November invades and closes the show.

***Sophie** – Monday, October 19, 1959. The school was closed today because of a big storm headed this way. I went outside early this morning, and it was as if time and all of nature had paused – perhaps to take inventory or prepare before an upheaval. There was no movement. No sound. No signs of life. And later, it suddenly rained – hard. The wind blew the bird feeders out of the trees and knocked over some backyard patio furniture. But all was OK.*

***Sophie** – Friday, November 27, 1959. I finally got enough money together and had the film developed recently. I had forgotten what photos I had taken – so it was a great surprise to see pictures of Miss Ellie at her back-yard princess birthday party, my garden, two of Randal in his front yard one day, my bike, and even a terrible picture of Sinatra, the dog next door – he would not stay still long enough. After I showed them to Miss Ellie and allowed her to keep all she wanted, I will put all these and others I have taken in a box that I keep on the shelf in my bedroom closet – next to my schoolwork and yearbook – for safekeeping. They will keep fine there in the closet – no dust. I was thinking of putting some pictures in this diary - but this book is just about boring me. My life, which the world thinks it sees beyond this little book – is in the box on the shelf in my closet – next to all my favorite childhood books that Miss Ellie read to me. Those are my happy memories. Before I could read, I memorized each word on each* *page. I knew the spelling of words before first grade. Cinderella and Peter Pan were always my favorites, and the pictures in my head were so much more wonderful than those in the books. They were alone, like me, and waiting for salvation and escape. But Miss Ellie, however, could hardly ever be confused as an evil stepmother!*

Cindy – No such box of priceless pictures or favorite books was found when Walters passed away in 1972. All this and more were likely part of Walters's big bonfire in the backyard after Sophie left town.

Sophie *- Saturday, November 28, 1959. I had no ambition to do so much this morning beyond staying in bed. I want to wait for the sun to awaken the day fully. Until then, gravity has found a way to settle right here and hold me tight beneath my quilt. I thought about where and how your soul is being held. Is there a place to put it for safekeeping until life shows you the way out? Where can I park my memories, dreams, dark times, and places? I had my hand mirror under the covers with me so we could talk and share secrets and giggles.*

Sophie *- Saturday, December 5, 1959. A few kids have dropped out of school and started working in the lumber yards, ice shops, and turpentine business. They said they could make some money now by doing that. What drives one to sacrifice their future for meager rewards for the moment? My only hope lives* *within myself and the future – how can I make the best of it and, hopefully, somehow be remembered?*

Sophie *– Monday, December 7, 1959. It is incredible how self-centered people are - they seldom look or consider beyond their assumed reality. I am sure this is why we named our planet Earth when it is primarily made of water. But I suppose the ultimate example of such conceit is writing a diary!*

Cindy - I wanted to tell her that despite her non-existent gene pool, chaotic times, short life, and dysfunctional family, she found a glorious way to accomplish immortality within this diary. **How many adults and aging daughters get a first-hand view into the life and times of their mother's childhood to teenage years? This is not a collection of memories. This is her life as she saw and experienced it for the first time.** It is a treasure beyond all measure.

Sierra Sommers *- Friday, December 25, 1959. Tonight, with Sierra – There are koalas, kids, and wombats on Christmas night in Canberra, Australia. Her thoughts transfer into actions - anywhere and anytime without the restraint of time, place, or travel arrangements. **Sierra goes to where her thoughts and imagination fly.** According to Sierra, when we stop exploring, we stop living. She spends time playing games with Aboriginal children.*

Cindy – Interesting – nothing more of Christmas is mentioned this year.

Sophie *– Sunday, December 27, 1959. I went to church with Mrs. Williston. She is a bit unsteady on her feet at times. We talked about when she was my age and how she helped her mother.*

It occurred to me how much of an outcast I am. I am alone in a kingdom where everyone thinks they know my name. I am alone among friends who avoid talking to me about my Mother, sister, or father and exclude Miss Ellie like she is a pet. They all try to mean well. But they probably have many questions but also assume they already know everything, including gossip. I can feel it in every corner, side glance, and whisper. It makes the truth look very tame. And truthfully, I don't want to talk about it all and wish I had control and could make so much of it disappear. The only person who understands is Randal. He leaves the door open to listen. He asks how I am doing. He would protect anything I would say to him like no one else. But he is away and back at his school already --- and for years to come.

Perhaps I don't belong here anymore, and I should go someplace else to start over and escape and leave my past here.... If only there were such a place and family to go to. It would relieve me from always behaving as expected, not as I am. Sometimes, I am angry and feel I have no choices and question what madness the future has in store for us. Am I guilty of thinking I have been robbed of my childhood – and myself? Private school would be excellent – there would be no one to gossip, and no one would know us. I would be gloriously anonymous and could share what I wished with others, build my own life and existence, and determine what parts, if any, I want to share. My life would be private instead of a spectator sport. I want to be unknown and have a boring past. Even when I may feel "alone," I genuinely am not. She is with me as each of us protects the other. Always. Thankfully.

Cindy – I am not sure I understand some of this except to say Sophie sounds so lost and alone. I wondered if, at times, her escape from herself and her situation was to become Sierra.

Sophie *– Wednesday, December 30, 1959. The night beyond my bedroom window was so dark tonight – as if God had inhaled all light and sound, perhaps to recharge his imagination upon their splendor or deprive us of the glory as punishment for the frightful state we have made of the world.*

THE WEEDS IN WONDERLAND

Cindy - The 60s invaded Sophie's life simultaneously, as did her teenage years with all its love, peace, protest, and mayhem of racial unrest. The Vietnam War escalates. Further, women's liberation is making news, and *American Bandstand* and *Twilight Zone* are famous on TV.

1960 Brought with it:

- John F. Kennedy won the Presidency in 1961.

- Aluminum cans start showing up on market shelves.

- March 11, 1960 – Pioneer 5 Spacecraft launched from NASA.

- The songs - *Teen Angel* by Mark Dinning,

- *Poetry in Motion* by Johnny Tillotson,

- *Walk, Don't Run* by The Ventures, and

- Chubby Checker is doing *The Twist.*

Cindy – With some vague feeling of growing civil unrest, 1960 perhaps provided the first thought of discomfort with leaving the home's front door unlocked and kids safely walking unattended to school. While Peanuts comic strips and Golden books sell for 25 cents, The Lone Ranger provided the diversion and comfort of familiarity and order on television.

Sophie – *Monday, January 4, 1960. Happy birthday to Randal #19. I sent him a card to remind him in case he was too busy going to class and learning everything about chimpanzees and wombats to remember.*

Sophie – *Saturday, February 13, 1960 - I read about this in the newspaper today. Yesterday, a group of students from Euclid High School quietly protested by sitting at the lunch counter at Woolworths in downtown DeLand. Some were carrying signs. They knew that colored folks were not served there. After a while of being ignored, they walked away. I hear they went to McCrory's across Woodland Blvd. It was a peaceful sit-in to let the world see they wanted to be treated like anyone else. Is it true that their money does not work there? Really? Why, why, why...*

I need to talk to Miss Ellie about this. I am considering inviting these brave kids here for some bottles of Coca-Cola, cake, and maybe a few games – but father would likely disapprove.

Sophie – *Monday, February 15, 1960. I asked Miss Ellie why everyone was so concerned with skin color. Why can't we all be friends and be nice to one another? She said that she did not rightly know other than some folks are just scared of anything a bit "different." There are plenty of good colored folks who would help anyone anytime. Skin color is no good reason not to like and trust someone.*

I always see differences in nature – and it does not matter. A field of wildflowers can be all colors, heights, and sizes, and the butterflies there are also all different sizes, shapes, and colors, and all get along just fine. Nature finds a way to live together, tolerate and respect differences, and thrive. Red roses can grow in the same garden as yellow roses. At the pet shop, all the different puppies play together. The oceans, forests, and my backyard welcome all types and kinds of plants, birds, and more. Why can't people? Maybe we are the ones who don't belong here.

The more I see, the more I like all weeds more than many people. They find a way to live and grow among each other. They thrive without human intervention. There is no discontent among wildflowers - which appears to be more evidence that hate is a human creation.

Miss Ellie says she spoke with Pastor Rawls about the plight of poor people long ago. He was a very gentle and thoughtful man. He said the poor are like God's Houseplants. They live within His home, love, and care but are confined to a view of the world from His windowsill. They are kept in a long pot, reaching out and holding each other tightly with their roots. While they cannot frolic freely in the meadows or dance in the breeze, they grace that windowsill, share the sunshine, and reach their leaves to touch the sky – together.

Cindy – And then yet more poetic words graced the page...

***Sophie** – Sunday, Feb 28, 1960. Gentle sun beams descended upon the early morning Spring breeze and gently awoke my senses as a pink sky peeked into my window and painted my bedroom wall in pastel. The sky and trees reach out to each other in mutual appreciation. Morning is almost like a romance (I guess) between the earth and the heavens.*

*I saw Twilight Zone the other night. The episode was called **Mirror Image** - about a lady seen by others before – like she has a twin whom only others see. It reminded me of a study we did about doppelgangers recently. I love the show. Randal does, too. He once told me he enjoys "adoring the abhorring" – like Alfred Hitchcock. Miss Ellie says it just gives her the creeps. People believe what they want to see – in so many ways – even when truth and reality may be very different and hiding in plain sight.*

***Sophie** – Wednesday, March 9, 1960 – Happy birthday number 13! It is also Barbie Doll's birthday #1. So, while she may look more grown up, I am the teenager of the two of us! So, this is what it is like to be 13! So, put that into your plastic high heels, Barbie! I am a big bad teenager! My friends at school brought me some Sweet Tarts and Starburst candy from McCrory's after school today. Miss Ellie made me my favorite Red Velvet cake – we went to her home after dinner and shared it with her friends. father did not even say hello.*

***Sophie** - Tuesday, April 5, 1960. – We went to **Marineland**! We took a bus ride from school with my science class. It is a bit south of St. Augustine on the ocean. What a wonderful, wonderful place. Sierra Sommers would love it! She is interested in and wants to see and do just about everything! Next, I think she will explore the Caribbean islands – and learn to sail a boat. Then, maybe she will swim with some dolphins. We learned about some places in Social Studies – so she has added the following to her list of places to go: Machu Picchu, take a boat ride in Venice, and see the caves of Lascaux in France. When I develop my pictures, I will put one here, and the rest will go into my collection in my closet.*

Marineland June 1962 CO39057.
https://www.floridamemory.com/items/show/80049

Cindy – Sophie writes about music, television, movies, dances, and sharing social interests with friends throughout the diary. Socially, she mimicked a butterfly in the garden, flitting from here to there, seldom in one place long. She also mentions ticket stubs, dried flowers, yearbooks, pictures, receipts, schoolwork, books, letters, clothing, and more. All Walters likely burned and allowed the ashes to flee and vanish among the Florida breeze later – all except for this diary.

Sophie – Thursday, April 21, 1960. I was thinking - perhaps life is merely a vacation respite for Angels such as Miss Ellie. Their chance is to experience a different life, share their innate wisdom, and challenge mere mortals to do better. Or maybe it is also an opportunity for them to experience and better understand the power of greed, evil, racism, or poverty.

Sophie- Sunday, April 24, 1960. I got my backyard garden all planted. In addition to the usual veggies, I want to grow a bunch of Sunflowers. I look forward to having plenty of sunflower seeds for the Cardinals this year. Plus, I love the flowers – they are so bright and sunny that you can't help but smile! I tried to plant enough vegetables this year that the rabbits could not eat them all, and I got some, too. And the morning sunshine makes young turkey feathers iridescent in the breeze.

Cindy – Sophie continued to grow – quickly. Her interests were shifting to Women's liberation, radicals, and Hippie unrest. She wrote, "I hope the world is at peace when I die."

She also started questioning more about the world closer to home:

On Saturday, April 30, 1960, she wrote: *"father says that church is just a place where people are made to feel good, so it is easier to con them out of their money.*

Sophie *– Sunday, May 1, 1960. Why is the Church the only place to promote good and kindness? Miss Ellie says if each person did something nice for another person daily, the world would have no war, less hunger, and more happiness.*

Last week, I went to church with Miss Ellie across from her home. I met the kindest people on the planet. Concern for others is their life and what they do every day. Pastor tells us about heaven and where there is love and happiness. He said goodness and joy live in gentle comfort, times, and places. I wonder if that gets dull throughout all eternity. I prefer to become part of the great collective genius with the Master Creator. I believe Hell exists because, without evil, good would lack definition. Light requires the dark as much as darkness best shows the light.

Sophie *– Thursday, May 5, 1960. Some girls want to marry a doctor, run away with a Rock Band, or become a secretary for a big organization. I prefer to live as Sierra – an adventurous, independent, free spirit in the wind - free to travel all space to connect with all* *souls across all time. Ok – or maybe a Botanist will find a way to cover all of Nevada with wildflowers and azaleas. I wonder how I can channel Sierra and learn from her. I wonder what secrets she keeps and what I have in common with her. The long-elusive echoes I've heard for decades resonate within me.*

Cindy – Sometimes, days go by without an entry in her diary. Some of the ones she wrote were just random thoughts without much context. She mentions her inner soul, confidence, soulmate, prodigy, and Muse-- and then there are the fireflies, poison apples, rags to beauty, and a savior from it all. She was on the precipice between childhood and emerging adulthood. And then – reality makes it into her life.... Once again.

Sophie*- Tuesday, May 24, 1960. I came home from school, and father yelled and pushed me against the wall! I ran outside to find Miss Ellie carrying bags of groceries. She told me to stay outside with her until my father calmed down. Later, Miss Ellie checked the locks she had put on my bedroom door. "In this room, you should be safe she said, and if you are still afraid, you can use your rope ladder to get out of your window if you need to. She told me to go to Dr. and Mrs. Peterson's home if my father misbehaved and to call Miss Ellie. She said, "You shouldn't be around your father if he is mad and crazy. You come up here and lock your door and be quiet." SS*

Sophie – Tuesday, May 31, 1960. At school, Gayle told a few of us girls about how she helped the Medic and her mother in the back of the ambulance when her little brother was born two days ago. He could not wait to get to the hospital. So, they stopped the ambulance on the way, and boom - there he was to greet the Medic and Gayle. Her brother is doing great, and her mother says she is so proud of how Gayle helped and knows she will be a great Nurse – or maybe even a doctor someday!

Sophie – Saturday, June 4, 1960. Miss Ellie asked me about my weed garden in the backyard. I explained that when weeds show up in my front garden, where I plant annual flowers, I thank them for visiting and gently dig them up. Then, I transplant them to the plot in the backyard so they can be among their friends near the *woods. I feel sorry for the lone weed that finds itself among stranger plants and lost and alone through no fault of its own. Besides, it is how nature beats the Grim Reaper and finds eternal permanence in continual rebirth and replacement – you need to be near your kind to make that happen. Survival makes the most of each opportunity when you are an unloved weed.*

Miss Ellie shook her head. "Apologizing to the weeds. Oh Lord, please love this child."

I told her that hope grows in gardens of all types.

Sophie *– Tuesday, June 7, 1960. Miss Ellie taught me a bit of needlepoint today –she got me this kit for my birthday. I started it a few weeks ago, but she showed me how to do better. I am working on a beautiful picture of a flower garden. I will show it to my plants in the front yard when I finish the needlepoint – maybe my flowers will get the idea!*

Sophie *- Today, I mentioned to Miss Ellie about a new girl named Jonna at school. I am not sure she heard anything I said after that. Miss Ellie told me girls deserve their own name – not a boy's name with an A at the end. Girls named Roberta, Erica, and Willa make me think they disappointed their Mama when they were born a girl. There is nothing fair about that.*

Sophie *– Tuesday, June 14, 1960. I asked Miss Ellie; please tell me about my mother in a quiet moment between us two. I shall try to quote her here.*

"Miss Sophie - I did not rightfully ever meet her. It is only what others have told me." She paused as if waiting for me to change the subject, but on the contrary, I did not want to interrupt her in any way. "She was a pretty, kind, and smart lady from out of town. She had no brothers or sisters. It seems she had not much in the way of remains of any family. If I have my facts right, she was not from these parts but from up north. Somewhere, I heard she played piano very well. So much as you do."

"Please tell me more," I asked. Miss Ellie said, "The truth needs to stay buried and left undisturbed. Leave it be. Unfortunately, the truth and happiness aren't always best friends, and I don't repeat gossip."

So, I asked her to tell me about her mother.

Miss Ellie was quiet for a moment before she sat down. "My mother passed when I was just a bit older than you were when your mother passed. We were new to Florida and had been here a few weeks when she got very sick and died in her sleep.

"But I remember her being kind and smiling at me. She worked hard but sat on the floor with me and played. When she passed, many church people helped and took turns ensuring I grew up right and had what I needed. I stayed in different homes for several weeks – all were nearby, as was the school. I got to meet, love, and be loved by everyone there."

Sometimes, I feel like a forgotten houseplant about to fall off the windowsill and crash unnoticed onto the dirt. Soph

***Sophie** - Thursday, June 16, 1960. I asked Miss Ellie, "Why do people tell me that poor people are so lazy, and why don't they go to school and get good jobs?" Miss Ellie stopped putting away dishes, took a deep breath, and said, "Where do you hear this, and where do I begin? Let me show you. I want you to meet some of them. You come to church with me this Sunday, and we will meet some wonderful people. Tell Mrs. Williston you can't attend church with her this weekend."*

She took a moment but continued to put away clean dishes and fold laundry. When she finished, we sat down at the table on the back porch, and she said, "Come over this way. Here are just a few great people to tell you about:

"I will take you to meet Durant. He is about 48 years old. He stopped school in fifth grade because his father needed help chopping wood and crating oranges to make enough money to feed his two young sisters and his mother. His father died when the chopping axe nearly cut off his leg. He has been doing his father's work ever since. He never had a chance to go back to school. Sometimes, he would work all night to see his children as they walked by his shop on their way to school in the morning. He is so proud of them. One

goes on to college next year. He also cares for the church and grounds - but there is no pay.

"And then there is "Bessie Gram." She is a great-grandmother to 10 children. She also takes care of the children of women who can find work – but it mostly does not pay well enough for childcare. So, for 40 years, Bessie has been watching over boys and girls (and eventually their children), taking them to the playground, teaching them Bible verses and songs, cleaning up the town of trash, and watering flowers in the park. They also help to deliver donated food to local elder folks who cannot cook. She won't take any money as long as working mothers put some money each month into a college account for their child. Because of Bessie Gram, working mothers today can help pay for a child or two to get a degree one day. Women like Miss Bessie are changing the world.

"Dear Old Mr. Will has been repairing shoes ever since I can remember. And he is the smartest man I know. He can fix anything – and I do mean anything. He knows everyone in town and how to get anything done. He is kind and generous, and at some time, he has saved the day for each person who lives here. One night, about 20 years ago, a bunch of white high school boys beat him up and left him for dead on the road. His leg did not heal straight, so he has some walking problems. But he finds a way to smile every day. Mr. Will saw that I got my first pair of real new shoes when I was six. I still remember them.

"They each have changed the lives of so many others. They each have sacrificed their future because they were needed in the now. These are great people you will never read about in history books but will live in our community's hearts forever. They make life better for others every day.

"Do you think they were lazy or too dumb to attend school? Or are these excellent, hard-working people sacrificing their future to help others? Life is never entirely fair for anyone, Sophie. But we each find a way to get through it. And between make-believe fairy tales and the struggle to live are stories of real people who changed the world for all who grace it today. "Nobody can live without help from others. Nobody. You realize how connected we are and how much we owe to history and those we never met. Each of us plays an important part in something or someone. It is not about where you came from or a future you may never see. It is also about doing good with what you have right NOW. That is where you permanently live.

"Poor people will do anything to get you what you need. But wealthy folks give their children what they want, and often, they don't do a good job of giving them what they need. And some folks are willing to pay more for what they want than they need. The differences between white and colored folk don't exist – it is only about where you see the good instead of imagining the bad.

"Good isn't all about going to church – it is about doing good for another daily. It is also about seeing the good in others every day. And not only is it good for others, but it also makes you a happier person to notice the good everywhere." She leaned back in the chair, took a deep breath, and closed her eyes briefly.

"Fairy tales tell you about the good times that last forever and ever. Miss Sophie, there is no forever. There is just NOW."

Miss Ellie says the unfairness of life is that "so many people think rich, good-looking people are all good folks- and sometimes that is true. But plenty of fat and not-so-pretty people who are much better and kind. That is where you often find comfort, kindness, and wisdom."

I don't think I have ever heard her say so much at once. I thought she was out of breath from talking so much at once – or perhaps gathering some courage to say more.

She then said something I did not expect but was true. "White people don't trust us with their belongings, but they will put the most important things to anyone – the precious lives of their children and elders - into our hands to take care of. And for that, I am most grateful and honored – but also bewildered. We live for, with, and because of our families. That is everything, and all that life is about where I come from. I guess that is just how we are raised."

"Miss Sophie, do you think I am lazy or dumb?" she asked.

"No, ma'am! You are the kindest, smartest, greatest person in the world, and I love you with all my heart and soul, Miss Ellie. Please realize that! I owe you the world. I don't understand why the rest of the world is so set in their ways not to see the plain truth around them," I meant every word I said.

She asked me to come to her and gave me an enormous, long hug I did not want to let go of. "You too smart to follow the crowd, Miss Sophie. You must tell people that we don't bite, will you? We need all the help to show we are good people, like themselves in many ways."

Sophie *– Sunday, June 19, 1960. I went to church with Miss Ellie today. After the service, she walked me a few blocks to meet each person she had told me about a few days ago. Each was glad to meet me. They were kind, humble, polite, and poor in worldly possessions but rich in spirit. They smiled, shared stories, and showed me pictures of their children and grandchildren. I also met Elmond, who has been cutting hair since he was eight and had to stand on a chair. Today, Elmond is an old man. His Father was determined that he would have a skill he could use for life. He taught him how to cut hair and shave beards, and he has done that nearly every day since. Everyone was warm, kind, and thoughtful. There was no hate. Life throws all sorts of things at you – what is so*

amazing is how people find a way to get through it all.
Sophie

Sophie *– Monday, July 4, 1960. Randal and his parents, Max the dog, Miss Ellie, and I will go to their home tonight for music, watermelon, and fireworks from the front porch. Randal is home for a holiday and returns to college soon. At first, the loud noise from the fireworks scares Max – but he gets over it quickly. I held him for a while until he felt safe. Randal played his guitar, and we sang and danced as he played "The Twist" by Chubby Checker.*

Sophie *– Saturday, August 20, 1960. Wow, 8th grade. For some reason, I can't get excited about that. I want to become a travel photographer and follow Sierra wherever she goes. Today, she is contemplating what she can do in South America. She is thinking about what she learns from children without understanding their language:*

"They taught me how to play a game with sticks and stones today. The city here has a building with clear windows. I have some blank paper, tape, and pencils with erasers. I also have black-and-white stretches of trees, flowers, animals, children, kittens, and more for them to copy. So, I taped the sketch on a sunlit window, placed a blank white page over it, and had them sketch the image on the blank paper. Then we made leaf rubbings, and one child found a dead snake – so we drew a picture of that, too. I brought out my magnifying glass so they could see its scales and details. They are

very interested in it all. We have a wonderful time. Love is the universal language that crosses all time and space and echoes through eternity." Sierra

Sophie *– Sunday, September 11, 1960. Hurricane Donna came uninvited to visit us today. It was an angry storm determined to make a mess of anything possible. Fortunately, we got through it well. Others saw a lot of damage. It is a mystery why they insist on naming these storms after women. They say it is because the storms (supposedly like women) are unpredictable. Hurricanes are destructive and violent and leave a mess behind. No woman would leave things like this without cleaning up first. After things quieted down, I went to check on Mrs. Williston and told her I'd clean up her yard after school tomorrow – but then some big trees came down at school. So now we have no class for a couple of days. S*

Sophie *– Saturday, September 24, 1960. Donna sent her friend Florence to visit us today. Florence was just a bit of wind and rain – and all threat with no fury. Not a big deal at all.*

Sophie *– Tuesday, October 25, 1960. I often dream of being in a big train station with tracks and signs for various destinations. Someone asks me, "Where are you going?" and I never have an answer.* ***I have no idea where I am going or how to get there. And then I wake up to find myself at home - alone. I feel both captive and abandoned. S***

Cindy – Oh wow – how many times have I awoken in a panic attack in the middle of the night amid a similar scenario in a large, crowded airport with thousands of people all around? I am repeatedly asked, "Where are you going – what is your final destination?" But, of course, where you are going also begs whether you have an answer as to why you are going there. My standard response in the dream has been, "Nowhere."

Sophie – Sunday, October 30, 1960. Halloween has been a favorite event for me for years. Happy times and places of scary moments and faces! People would come up with the most creative costumes! I loved walking downtown with friends in costume. As the years have passed, fewer children have come to my home hoping to get candy for trick or treat. It seems the neighbors are afraid my father will frighten them away, and the night he passed out in the front yard naked is a story (and sight) that I can't get out of my head. Apparently, they have the same affliction. SS

Cindy – Some of her posts entered the realm of philosophical and beyond personal social concerns. She was infringing more upon women's liberation, racial inequality, and the insanity of war.

Sophie – Saturday, November 5, 1960. I was helping to dust the furniture and told Miss Ellie, "I live to dream. Someday, I wish to be with those I want to be with."

Miss Ellie responded, "And while you live to dream, I dream to live. Someday, I pray that everyone is equal, respected, and treated fairly."

Miss Ellie, our goals are much alike – but we appear to be attacking them from different sides. S

***Sophie** – Saturday, November 19, 1960. There was a car accident last night. Two students died at the scene on Kepler Road near New Daytona Road. They were both seniors about to graduate from my school. Rod was 18, and Sheila was going to be 18 in December. Even though they both attend this school, and I know I have seen them, neither was in my classes. Some Seniors were crying in the hallway. It is so unfortunate. Rod planned to fly planes for the Air Force. He was driving fast with her in the car when they ran off the road, and the vehicle rolled over in the ditch.* **We are too young to die – doesn't God, all of Mother Nature, and the angry world of machine guns see that? The future of everything is dying.** *Who watches over things when God and his Angels are sleeping? I will hug Miss Ellie tomorrow morning – and might not let go for a few years. Sophie*

Miss Ellie asked me later today, "Why do young, wealthy white high school kids with everything in life risk it all like that? "

I have no answer.

***Sophie** – Sunday, November 20, 1960. Why do people die? What is the point of living only to have it* *taken away from you? At least most people cannot foresee when or how they will die, so it does not seem to be something you can plan for or schedule a time for, so you won't be alone when your soul disappears into the beyond. How cruel to give you life and swoop down and repossess it at will and randomly. If it is mandatory that you MUST die, I would appreciate the opportunity to say goodbye and thank you to those who made my life better. When I asked Miss Ellie why people suddenly die, she said it makes life much more important and reminds us to love each other better. Dying, she said, is easy. It is the living part that is so hard at times. Sophie*

Sophie *– Monday, November 21, 1960. Everyone at school is still quiet and sad about the car accident that killed those students. Some girls were crying in the bathroom. I did not know these students; I just saw them in the hallways. Then I think about how I would feel if those were friends of mine. I would cry, too.*

To make matters worse, the bomb scares at school are scary and becoming so frequent that everyone walks outside in line like mindless trained monkeys, and no one even talks anymore. School teaches us good information – science, art, music, history, homemaking, sports – but we live in a life of reality – hate, crime, violence, alcohol, lies, and deceit -- what prepares us for that? **Where is the right in a sea of so wrong?**

Sophie *-Thursday, December 2, 1960. Maybe I am the spirit of two attracted to one another like opposite magnets. It seems to be only then that I am complete. Where my adventurous meets my cautious, my studious joins up with the social, and each is scared and feels alone. And each with equal determination – and menacing thoughts of a meaningless and short life...*

Sierra and Ethics – Heaven, is it real or just a tragedy of optimism and made-up incentive to keep people nice? If there was no reward for being good, would some do it anyway, or would evil deeds and selfish greed to immediately collect the most of everything now be the only goal for everyone? And how can there be light without darkness? How can you experience joy without also experiencing pain?

Miss Ellie says the law keeps folks from killing one another – in theory, anyway. But no law can explain what is good. Good keeps us going and appreciating each other forever. Doing bad might bring happiness for a moment. Good is planting the seeds of plants that we may never see that show love for each other forever. And despite how hard evil tries, it can never kill the belief in hope and good in people.

Miss Ellie said, "Each day, try to make the world a bit better – even if I only smile at a child or thank God for the sunshine. Try to fill your life with enough love to share with all - then there is no room for gossip."

So, in such situations, I wonder what Sierra would do. SS

Sophie *– Monday, December 12, 1960. I can't be bothered this year with putting the Christmas tree up. I closed the drapes so the neighbors would not question the lack of a tree. I just can't. Plus, they look so pathetic, unloved, abandoned, and literally "kicked to the curb" on the side of the road once Christmas is over. I think it is the first time I have considered becoming Jewish. I made a needlepoint picture of a dog who looks like Sinatra with a Christmas bow on his head for Mrs. Williston and cookies for some friends, Randal, and Miss Ellie. I bought Max a new rubber ball to throw in the backyard. Downtown looks great, and the parade was fun with Millie and her family.*

Sophie *- Friday, December 16, 1960. Today, at school, they made snide comments to me regarding my Negro friends. I cried when I told Miss Ellie about it. They called me names because I sang Christmas Carols with her and some church folks in her neighborhood a few days ago. I asked Miss Ellie what did I do wrong?*

She said, "Child, it's my fault. I forget about folks out there who are afraid to see the truth. Their eyes cannot see what their heart does not allow. You did nothing wrong. You are brave, and that scares them. Hold your head up high and be proud. You are special, and they aren't. When you can't think of anything good to say, let your feet do the talking as you turn and walk away".

Where common folk lack in luxury, they shine in wisdom. Sophie

Sophie – *Tuesday, December 20, 1960. Randal and I went to see "The Time Machine" at the Athens and then off for a malt and some pizza. Downtown is all decorated for the holidays, and people are smiling everywhere! The movie was very good! Afterward, we talked about his classes and how he was adjusting to life so far away. Because of our age difference, I told people I did not know he was my older brother - or some such story. He played along well with it! While I would never tell him this - I would love for him to be my brother. For starters, maybe he would be here to help when father was on the floor in the mornings and before Miss Ellie arrived. S*

Sophie - *Sunday, December 25, 1960. Randal gave me a bunch of Bic Ballpoint ink pens! I love them and have used a few for a while. He says he does not understand how he wrote papers and homework without them. He heads back to college on Thursday this week. S*

Sophie – *Saturday, Dec 31, 1960. Fireworks are booming tonight – poor Max is probably going to be terrified – and PC is leaving late this afternoon to get back to his classes. I think I will ask if Max can stay with me tonight. I can sneak him in the backdoor, so father does not see him. Max will be less scared with me when the loud booms go off later tonight. ss*

Cindy – I read this last diary entry to Jonathan and asked, "Who is PC?" He thought for a moment before a smile came to his face. "Sophie used to call me Prince Charming," he said.

THREE WISHES

Some Highlights of 1961 include:

- John F. Kennedy became President of the United States.

- John B. Stetson University purchased a massive Beckerath Organ for the Elizabeth Hall Chapel. It arrives from Hamburg, Germany, in 56 crates.

- The US sent troops to Vietnam.

- *Runaway* is a popular song by Del Shannon.

- Walt *Disney's Wonderful World of Color* is on TV.

- **Antonio Peterson** was born on February 3, 1961.

- New DeLand High School on Plymouth & Hill Avenue opened in December 1961.

Cindy – It was a time of peace, conflict, and change colliding with tradition along a rapid undercurrent of uncertainty in all directions. The war in Vietnam was invading the news and disrupting the social consciousness.

Sophie – Sunday, January 1, 1961. Finally, a new day of the new year starts on the first day of a new week! With a clear blue sky high above, the grey clouds are held up by branches of stoic tree limbs struggling to defend the cold soldiers trudging through the heartless winter below. Christmas was the only saving grace of winter, and it comes too early in winter to lighten the tired souls of late January and early February for those so unaccustomed to the cold. However, the South shall rise again! (All right – confession – I am unsure how those words made it into this! Besides Blue & Grey and Confederates, they are marching through my brain after reading the school history assignment. I apologize to my own diary!)

Sophie *– Wednesday, January 4, 1961. Randal is 20! Darn – he is getting old! I sent him a birthday card, but it seldom arrives on time because of the New Year holiday.*

Cindy - Some entries were just snippets of imagery and thought. For example, on Saturday, January 7, 1961, Sophie wrote, "*The darkness lingers unabated longer into the morning and seems anxious to return earlier each evening as if the sun was playing hooky from its daily duty to chase the gloom away from the sky. Gravity may imprison me to the planet - but not to this house. But first, it simply must warm up before I get out of bed!*" Sophie

Sophie *– Saturday, January 18, 1961. Miss Ellie needed a bit of time to "vent" today. She said, "Men may get all the credit for being the breadwinners, but the women put in the endless hours and work the hardest and the longest. Yet, men have the domain over the recliner chair and the television set that* *extends well beyond any hope of leisure for women. When will they realize how hard we work, too?" SS*

Sophie *– Wednesday, February 1, 1961. I was notified that Mrs. Henries, a long-time school counselor, wanted to meet me at 1:00 today. My teacher had already excused me from that class so I could talk with her. I asked my teacher what it was about – was I in trouble? She said, No - Mrs. Henries likes to speak with students and determine their interests.*

I went to her office in the school at 1:00, as requested. She is a lovely lady who has been here forever. We talked about how I was doing (OK), what I liked in school, and my plans. I told her I like science – plants, animals, and astronomy.

She asked what I knew about caring for myself – cooking, shopping, sewing, washing, etc. I told her Miss Ellie is great about showing me anything. Then, she asked if Miss Ellie was my colored lady. I answered before stopping and saying, "Miss Ellie isn't my colored lady. She is my friend and the kindest and wisest person on the planet." I was instantly annoyed, ashamed, and proud of myself for being so blunt with an adult.

Mrs. Henries changed to another question. "Can you tell me who is your hero?" So, I told her about my memorized list of people I wanted to meet when I passed on. Anne Sullivan, Amelia Earhart, Leonardo di

Vinci, Michelangelo, and Emily Dickinson – and maybe Walt Disney and I wish to become friends with Anne Frank. And I have a few questions for God – there is so much I don't understand.

Mrs. Henries smiled. "That is a great list! But why is Mr. Disney on the maybe list?"

"Because I was determining if he was more motivated to spread joy or to make money."

She asked, "What might be your biggest question in science?"

I thought a second and said, ***"How did one planet, among other planets and millions of stars and bits of rock, make the leap to having plants, animals, bacteria, butterflies, and rainbows?"***

She smiled again. "Sophie, I wanted to talk to you to see if maybe I can work on getting you a scholarship to Princeton University. They have a great program for Natural Sciences. How does that sound to you? I can't make any promises, but I will work on it if it sounds like something you want to do," she said.

I was surprised and thrilled! "YES, I would! John B. Stetson does not look like it offers anything I am good with or have much interest in. Although, they have some rocks and minerals, a music program, and their library has some horticulture information."

Mrs. Henries said, "Princeton has zoology, botany, and biology classes, and I am glad you mentioned libraries! But remember that a scholarship will apply after you graduate from high school and if you keep your grades up! And it may take many months and maybe a year before we are notified if you get it!"

I said, "That is OK. I'm not going anywhere."

She said, "In the meantime, get active in the National Honor Society as soon as possible. I also have a book I found, and I think you will enjoy it. It is about a young lady who finds a way to survive on an island. I have a copy here for you. Please read it and let me know what you think of it. Also, I think our library has a book about Amelia Earhart. I will ask Miss Jones to get it to you."

I thanked her, and then she asked if I had any questions.

"When can colored students and girls be as important as the boys? For example, I want to take Shop Class and make things rather than home economics." I asked.

Mrs. Henries paused for a moment. "I think I understand what you mean. If so, Sophie, that is a big question, and I wish I had the answer. But someday, I am sure it will happen. So please hang in there --- and do me a favor - go to college when you graduate high school!"

The book she gave me is "Island of the Blue Dolphins" by Scott O'Dell – it is the story of a 12-year-old girl alone on an island for years. She got separated from her family. Before school was over for the day, Miss Jones brought me the book about Amelia Earhart from the library.

I decided then to wait to tell father anything about the potential scholarship. I don't think he ever went to college, and I am unsure how he will react.

From there, I went to an English class with Mr. Jenkins teaching. He stood before the class and said to everyone, "Write, people! Write! I want to see your daily Journals by this Friday. Put into writing what you think and are feeling. You don't understand anything until you put it into words that resonate with others. Only one student here is improving in transforming thoughts into words – and she is just now walking into the classroom! Miss Sherman!" I was a bit stunned and embarrassed, and at the same time, it felt good. First Mrs. Henries, and now this. On the same day. Wow!

Yes, I write my Journal daily as Mr. Jenkins requests. Sometimes, I don't write in my diary as a result, and sometimes, I use what I wrote in my diary as part of my journal. But what I provide Mr. Jenkins is carefully crafted to avoid inside info. I do not share my family world with anyone besides Miss Ellie and this diary. For Mr. Jenkins, I write about general injustice and the order and logic of the natural world vs. the madness and damage of society. The outside world and daily newspapers bring plenty of fodder into question regarding the single contributing misfit factor so out of place in this world – people. At times, I include the dreams and adventures of Sierra Sommers. At one point, he even wrote back and suggested I make Sierra less "gender generic" (I had to look that one up in the dictionary) and keep her smile, long hair, small comforts, and mannerisms. She puts flowers into the hair of children and women. She is still female – make sure to keep that – while she flies a plane, hikes a mountain, and makes friends with a llama!

Cindy – I had to stop and wonder, how does this vibrant young lady with so much promise end up alone at the bottom of the stairs of an abandoned building nearly 60 miles away just two years later? And for the first time, I was not anxious to find out. I prefer to keep her as she is here – forever.

Sophie *– Thursday, February 2, 1961. Last night, I dreamed Sierra had brought her horse, Amelia, to my home. I rode her through the neighborhood. She is a beautiful chestnut color with a white mane and socks. I could feel the wind through my hair, and the thrill of adventure was just ahead. Sierra longs to sail the Bahamas and plant something that will live for generations. This morning, I noticed I had left one window slightly open. The breeze likely contributed to the realism of the dream!*

Sophie *– Friday, Feb 3, 1961. Antonio Peterson was born! I have not seen him yet, but I was told he is* *adorable. He has dark curly hair and hazel eyes. Randal is his uncle, and he looks forward to showing him how to play guitar. Antonio and his family live nearby – about two miles away. I am not sure exactly where, however. I want to get a picture of him and send it to Randal.*

I plan to read the book Mrs. Henries loaned me this weekend by O'Dell. My first impression was about a damsel in distress, and I wonder if that is how Mrs. Henries sees me. ***I think of myself more as the princess guarding the palace. I am a beloved untouchable in a kingdom where everyone calls me Sophie – but I am alone among my friends who will not talk to me about my mother, sister, or father and exclude Miss Ellie as an abnormality.*** *I cannot share such things with others who would not understand and only see my weaknesses anyway.*

Cindy – It is exciting and funny to read about present-day Antonio when he was young. In so many ways, he still has an endless supply of wonder and youth within him. The same applies to reading about Randal as an ambitious and intelligent young man who has become my wise, supportive friend in Jonathan.

Sophie *– Thursday, March 9, 1961. Happy birthday, number 14! I put some petunias around Miss Ellie's Magnolia tree. We planted it when I was nine years old. I also put a small white picket fence around it. I'll water it all every morning until the afternoon thunderstorms start to show up in a few months. I remember that Miss*

Ellie named the Magnolia "Angel Tree" because its two branches, at that time, resembled wings and currently appear as arms reaching for the heavens.

Early today, a redheaded woodpecker was in the tree, yammering loudly about some injustice in his world. Some days, I wonder if anyone is happy anymore.

Sophie *– Friday, March 10, 1961. – Happy "day after my birthday" day to me! I took a driver's test after school today. father arranged for me to have the Studebaker – he bought a new Ford for himself. Miss Ellie will ride when I drive as my mentor. So, we have been riding along the community roads at times. I am learning how to convince her to go shopping for anything. I like to entice her with ice cream from Winn-Dixie so I can drive. It is a good but old car – a 1954 Land Cruiser that is maroon with a white top and four doors. Miss Elie thinks it is the snazziest car ever! Mr. O'Reilly, father's Accountant, gives me an allowance for school supplies, clothes, chewing gum, and things. He increased it to pay for gasoline in the car, and he paid for the insurance and repairs. He puts the money in my bank account every two weeks. Miss Ellie packs my school lunch – so I don't spend much money.*

Sophie *– Saturday, March 18, 1961. I saw the world as a much smaller child again today. I babysat for Arnold and Kate. Mrs. Werther asked if I could look after them while she did some shopping. Great little rug rats! Arnold is almost four years old and calls me*

"Soapy" and is constantly moving all the time! His sister is eight months old and watching his every move.

I enjoyed building and knocking down Towers of blocks as Arnold laughed out loud. I also got the finer points with formula, bottles, diapers, rocking chairs, and nursery rhymes. I made some money. Maybe I'll take Miss Ellie to visit the animals at the zoo in Sanford. She said she always wanted to see the monkeys. Me too. A few monkeys might revitalize her spirit. I should be able to pay for the gas and maybe a soda for each of us without taking money from my bank account. I so love animals. It is a toss-up between zoology and horticulture, although plants seem easier to get along with. Soapy

Sophie *- Saturday, March 25, 1961. Miss Ellie and I got into the car and took her to the Sanford Municipal Zoo by Lake Monroe. Big Goldfish, monkeys, Leo the Lion, a raccoon, and more. It was fantastic! At first, they did not want to let Miss Ellie in. I told them she was my Nurse and must come with me for medical reasons. Finally, they said they would allow it since it was a quiet day with few other visitors. I paid for both of us to enter. Miss Ellie had tears in her eyes. Why do I have to lie? In short order, we had fun. Miss Ellie laughed out loud – and in public, for the first time, I think, in her life! Later, we sat by the lake, drank a Coke, and ate some cookies I had brought. It was a great day!*

Monkey Island, Sanford, Fl. PR295150
https://www.floridamemory.com/items/show/340562

Sophie *- Monday, March 27, 1961. – Azaleas are blooming EVERYWHERE! Pink, purple, white, and red. I love this time of year as Mother Nature takes over the exterior decorating with such flare. I drove Miss Ellie around the neighborhood so she could see the flowers and I could practice driving. She had never been to Sugar Top on Amelia Ave – so I drove her out that way, too. I ordered two hamburgers that were delivered to my car.*

In writing class, Jensa read her daily insight to all this morning. She wrote, "Morning awakens a gentle world to soft light, sound, and hope. It is such a contrast to the mess people make of the day."

It reminded me of something Miss Ellie said one day: "It is the same thing that is both everything right and everything so wrong with the world. People, Miss

Sophie. Just plain ole everyday people."

Sophie *– Saturday, April 8. Miss Ellie was very quiet, holding her left arm and slowly walking. I asked what was wrong. At first, she said, "I have waited a long time to be this old." She took a breath and then said reluctantly that Louis (her boyfriend) had taken the money she was saving to buy a lilac dress to wear at the wedding of a good church friend next week. Louis had to pay some gambling debts. "He gets mean at times when he drinks."*

I cannot understand how men can love a lady so much and then beat her! Why do men hate the women they love? And why can't women live without them? Why do they go back? And why do men expect to be pardoned? Miss Ellie tells me only that love is fabulous, fragile, and flawed. SS

Sophie *– Sunday, April 9, 1961. I asked Miss Ellie how you excuse terrible things that some people do. She told me of how her 6-year-old daughter was killed in 1949. Someone wearing a white sheet from the organization KKK left her dying child at her front door, along with some dead flowers, and rang the doorbell before running off. Her neck had been broken. Tears were in her eyes as she spoke.*

*That night, I asked my mirror - **How do I forgive God for allowing bad things to happen to children?***

Miss Ellie said that she asks God to live within her to help her forgive, forget, and show others the way to *virtue. **Great love comes at the cost of great pain.** Miss Ellie says life becomes meaningless without someone to care for. I care for my reflection – she is love, and I am hope. The bond between us is tight.*

"A diamond ring is pretty, but I would trade all of them to have my daughter back. There is no stronger bond than that between a mother and her child. But people are so blessed to have those they miss so much – even when it hurts so very, very bad. That is the cost of love. I would not trade that for anything," she said.

God, can you see me? Help is needed for Miss Ellie. Please. Thank you, Sophie Sherman

Sophie *– Monday, April 10, 1961. Today, I took Miss Ellie to the Jr. Service League of DeLand Thrift Shop to help me find a dress I could wear to a dance. But then I quietly asked Mrs. Roberts there to find the prettiest lilac dress to fit Miss Ellie.*

Miss Ellie whispered, "No, Louis will kill me."

"Then tell Louis it is my dress, and you are just borrowing it," I whispered back.

"Lord!" she said. "Nobody is gonna believe all this (she pointed to herself) could ever fit into anything your skinny size!" I thought a moment.

"Oh. I just remembered! That dress belonged to my mother. I remember it as clear as day." And nobody has seen her in quite a while.

Mrs. Roberts helped Miss Ellie find the perfect dress as her fears turned to tears.

Sophie *– Monday, May 8, 1961. On the way to school today, I noticed the gardenia blooms in the yard are wonderful! The camellias across the front of the yard almost outdo them. I cut a few gardenias for Miss Ellie to put on the dining room table. They smell glorious!*

Today, the school counselor, Miss George, asked to talk with me. She said a friend of mine shared that she was worried about me. I keep my bedroom door unlatched so my dog can bite my father when he comes into my room angry. And I try very hard not to make a sound when my father hits me - which makes him hit harder.

She said she was worried and asked if I was all right. She asked if she could help me. I stretched my long sleeves down and held the ends tightly in my hands. Why did I ever say that to anyone? What is wrong with me? It was just "girl talk" when some friends came over.

I told Miss George not to listen to what others say, and whoever said this never saw it happen. Any marks on me are from the work I do in my gardens. She asked if she could see them. For the first time, I told an adult, "No."

I wondered if I could go home. She said yes. The tears held until I got outside. Is this how things are supposed to be? I sat behind some trees and waited for school to let out and everyone to get by before completing my walk home alone and my thoughts to myself. They don't understand.

Sophie *– Friday, May 12, 1961. I asked Miss Ellie how she deals with white people. She said you treat them like they are sleeping cats. "If you step in front of the sleeping cat, they get up and get annoyed. But approach them from behind and step wide around them; you can sometimes get right by them without notice. So, they stay out of your way, and we don't bother each other.*

"I think they want us to leave each other alone - and if that is all we can do, it is good enough for me right now. But I hope we can find a way not to bother each other so much. There are some fine, good folks on both sides. We love our children too," she said.

Sophie *– Saturday, May 13, 1961. I was having a "down" day and asked Miss Ellie about the necessity of evil. Is the opposite required to bring light to the dark? She looked at me funny, turned her head a bit, and said, "Well, I don't think much about all that, but it does sound true. Opposite things need each other to work, I guess. I truly believe that **God trains his best Angels within the depths of Hell**. And if that is not the opposite, I don't know what is!"*

"Here is another truth," she said. "Time, Miss Sophie is the longest road between people who love one another."

Not that I ever needed further proof to declare Miss Ellie was indeed an Angel – this confirmed it.

Sophie *- Monday, May 15, 1961. Sierra Sommers is my alter ego. She simultaneously needs no one and longs for everyone. She is fiercely independent but greatly enjoys being with others. However, she doubts she can devote herself to one person or if that person could ever love her in return. All this drives her further off the beaten path and into the jungles and swamps of humanity. Amelia Earhart said, "Never interrupt someone doing what you said couldn't be done."*

I may put this into my Journal to see what Mr. Jenkins thinks.

Sophie *– Saturday, May 20, 1961. Miss Ellie and I have been playing gin rummy card game lately. It is great fun – and darn! She is good! I must work very hard and cross my fingers to beat her. And that does not happen very often! We play for pretzels, walk to the nearby park, and feed the birds and squirrels with them afterward. Soph*

Sophie *– Friday, June 2, 1961. I told Miss Ellie after school today that **I am living to dream** someday where I have friends who are not afraid to visit my home, and girls aren't accused of acting like boys to do interesting things. I want friends and, simultaneously, to be completely independent and self-sufficient – where I never must depend upon anyone.*

She said back, "And where you are living to dream, ***I am dreaming to live*** *where I can walk down the street without being frowned at, unafraid to say "good morning" to white folk, where I can go to a movie, or walk into a store and I can be trusted first without question. I want people everywhere to be treated as the good persons they truly are."*

"And people, Miss Sophie, will always need people. We are incomplete without family and friends. I always want to be surrounded by family and friends."

Sophie*- Monday, June 5, 1961. I like sleeping late and wearing Bermuda shorts each day while on summer vacation from school. I am reading books and playing with Max today. I am thinking of driving Miss Ellie for some malts. Today, Miss Ellie was "Waltzing" to some good music on the radio. She appeared quite happy and said, "Today, if I were God, we would not be within bodies to be judged – but be free spirits who speak in song without words," she said. "How wonderful that would be!"*

And she did not stop there. "If I were God, I would ensure that each sunrise also had the promise contained within a rainbow – for all to see."

OK – that is pretty darn mellow – even for the queen serene of unflappable.

Sophie *– Tuesday, June 6, 1961. I hope someday to teach my child how wise and kind Miss Ellie is. How she saved me from God only knows what, how never* *to underestimate any folks or the wonders they hold inside. My job is to pass on what I understand and inform those I encounter of the next generation. Miss Ellie told me once that each life echoes, touches, and changes another somewhere and at some time – perhaps years or even generations later -- and how very, very much we need one another. I can't imagine I can do anything that powerful and lasting – but she certainly has. Everything that makes us today results from the actions and thoughts of those who have gone before.*

And - I went to see Antonio today. He is intelligent and adorable and is growing up so fast!

Cindy – There was a shiver up my back. I felt she was reaching out, touching, and talking directly to me over decades.

Sophie *– Thursday, June 8, 1961. Randal is home from college for a bit. He is all so grown up! He is even growing a mustache! Sophie*

Sophie *- Friday, June 9, 1961. father yelled on the phone, "Isn't that what life is - taking advantage of others! Yes, buy them out and run them out of town. No one can lead or follow that gang of misfits. And rules and truth are for idiots! I want them out of my way and to leave me alone!"*

It was a feeling of doom in the air. Miss Ellie gently shook her head and said, "Everyone fights their own battle, Miss Sophie. Let it be. Things and people are not always what they seem to be. You don't know the whole story, and he does. Try to forget it and hope he does what is best." Ss

Sophie *- Monday, June 12, 1961. Summer break means spending more time with Miss Ellie. She would say, "At the end of the day, list what you are thankful for. It could be for a good meal, seeing an old friend, a great song you heard, or just that the day is finally done. But there is always something to be grateful for. It all comes down to seeing the good more than the bad. Good is everywhere but is shy and can hide or show in small bits and unlikely places. The trick is not to let it go by without notice. When you look for the good, God will ensure it finds you. It almost sounds like an "I SPY" game that God provides each day." sof*

Sophie *– Tuesday, June 13, 1961. I asked Miss Ellie if she was afraid of dying. She said we are spiritual beings just living as humans. That is why she is not scared of dying.*

I am going downtown with Betty to shop for a pool party she wants to have soon. I offered to help but told her I could not attend the party. She said that was all right. We bought a big watermelon at the market. I drove my car.

Sophie *- Saturday, June 17, 1961. The women keep things in the future, plan, dream, do, and prevent chaos.* ***While men build empires in the sky, women keep the necessary machinery going without***

fanfare, accolades, or often payment. *Without women, men would not have clean clothes, shiny shoes, meals, get bills paid, organize the process of life, or have teachers. They would not write letters, make phone calls, or tie their own tie. If you see a woman not working to benefit others, it would be because she has died!*

So, I considered writing my own fairytale for young girls where you are granted just one of three wishes:

- To be beautiful or

- Have lots of money, or

- Have the intellectual ability to provide for yourself in a testosterone-dominated world.

This defines and separates the path girls will take (or chase in some circumstances). If I am smart enough, I could get a job to make enough money to buy things (including perhaps surgery) to make me pretty – and not depend financially on others.

To me, that is where the joy also is. I want out of the kitchen, away from those who cannot see to whom they owe their comfort - especially those whose meal often comes from a bottle.

I drove Randal to a store to buy some class supplies and a malt at Woolworths. We talked about girls doing more than cooking and cleaning. He agreed that was unfair and that men are terrible at cooking and cleaning. However, he thought that someday, a lady would be president. Other countries have women as rulers. And doing his laundry has not killed him yet.

I told Miss Ellie about what Randal and I talked about. She had much more to say about the topic in general.

"Most men work hard, Miss Sophie. They dig ditches, build bridges, and move mountains. But they also get time to relax. Women work all the time. Even in their sleep, they plan meals and do laundry while the sun shines as they clean homes and tend to children. Women never rest. While men build empires, women work to hold it all together. It is the women who make it a better place.

"While it is not for me to question such things, I think God over blessed boys and men with too much desire for women. They are the most dangerous and selfish of all. There is just no need for so much of it, which gets teenage boys and girls and adults into much trouble. Miss Sophie, love and respect differ from what boys want at this age. Unfortunately, sometimes the devil takes over. You are a beautiful young woman; boys have a drive that can hurt you in many ways. Their urges are strong, and you must say no and not trust them when you are alone.

*"Be careful, Miss Sophie. Boys at this age have trouble controlling themselves, and the law isn't always much help. **While God was relaxing after creating***

the world, I suspect Satan reached down and put an extra dose of fire into the souls of young men.

"And boys and menfolk always want more money, cars, speed, girlfriends. But ladies want better. Better gardens, cleaner clothes, kinder friends, better recipes, and better-behaved children. Boys want what they want now. Ladies, have patience."

Wow. I did not see this response coming! Good advice, though – I guess.

Sophie *– Monday, June 19, 1961. Miss Ellie seems sad today. She said, "Used to be, I had not enough time for everything in life; currently, it feels like life has no time left for me."*

So, hoping to brighten her up, I told Miss Ellie about a book I read (quite a while ago – by Anne Frank). A girl wrote it about my age. She wrote, "How wonderful it is that nobody needs to wait a single moment before starting to improve the world."

Miss Ellie said, "That is one smart young lady! I try to do that - Lord knows I try, but the world is a big place. I hope this girl does great things someday."

I thought it would be cruel to tell Miss Ellie that the author, Anne Frank, died soon after writing it. She was brave in such an awful time, and her words still resonate today.

__Sophie__ – Saturday, July 1, 1961. Today, I asked Miss Ellie what love is. Is it my father giving me his old car or letting me live in his home and giving me an allowance --- although I am not sure he remembers about my allowance as it comes from his accountant – is that love?

Miss Ellie says love is losing yourself to thinking about others. Love is also praying and sending good thoughts to others. It allows you to share and feel the good beyond what others cannot see. It changes how you understand things – all things. It is endless, everywhere, and forever. It shows you the simple joys that make you so happy to be alive. It costs nothing to be kind and think kind of others. And it is someplace where many coloreds are richer than many white folks. We smile, hug, and laugh so much more often.

So, I asked her if father loved me. She says he does in a way only he can. Love is a language of deeds and thoughts and few words. And love and hope __are twins.__

Then, I asked her if there was proof that prayer works. She said, "I have seen belief sway more minds than proof. I have not seen prayer remove cancer or old age, but it works miracles at times, and more than anything, prayer changes those doing the praying – because they learn to love without limits," she said.

I asked if thinking of others is also prayer. For example - I worry about Mrs. Williston tripping over her small dog and falling.

Miss Ellie said – Did that worry for Mrs. Williston get you to remind her to be careful about that? (I nodded yes). That is showing you care – that is indeed love, Miss Sophie.

I told her father says the devil reaches down and marks some people.

*Miss Ellie took a deep breath. "**Love is intolerant of intolerance.** And there is no earthly love greater than that for your child. Does Mr. Walters love you? Yes. Does he show or say it? No. And – there are consequences to everything. So, let that be the lesson. Make sure the consequences are good ones in your life. And Miss Sophie – make sure to love yourself. You are a good, brave, strong, very smart young lady many look up to. And as for people that the devil may mark – love them too." S*

***Sophie** – Sunday, July 2, 1961. I was thinking while driving Mrs. Williston to church today. Am I a fraud for protecting the truth from everyone, or are they all frauds for creating and believing their gossip? Keeping secrets was even the theme of the sermon today. I look into the mirror – and see us waiting, afraid to grow up... and worrying about what will become of the other. Sometimes, it is too easy, and then other times, it is very painful, and I remind myself every day not to cry – no matter what. I am scared. Thank you, God, for Miss Ellie.*

***Sophie** – Tuesday, July 4, 1961. Randal brought out his "first oldest" guitar case and guitar. It was a gift from his dad many years ago. We sat on the front porch of his home with our feet up on the rails and with bottles of Coca-Cola, popcorn, and watermelon and sang songs with Miss Ellie, Max, the dog, baby Anthony, and Randal's parents. Randal wanted to give his guitar a final send-off before putting it in his closet and buying his new one tomorrow. I asked Randall to play me, "Fly me to the moon." Max and I tried to fly with fireflies in the yard. father is away at a meeting in Orlando tonight, so Melody, my friend from school, came over, and we had a sleepover in my house and made several containers of Jiffy Pop popcorn – and had a food fight with it. Soph*

***Sophie** – Monday, July 17, 1961. Randal had to get back to college yesterday. He is working at some lab practice. Meanwhile, this morning, Max, his dog, passed away. It made me very sad that I was not there with Max then. Max was a great dog and friend. Randal's parents buried Max in the backyard. I placed the toys we played with and some cut sunflowers over his grave and cried. I miss him already.*

***Sophie** – Sunday, August 13, 1961. After church, Miss Ellie and I danced to the music on the radio - we talked about music as we changed the sheets. She likes a group called the Platters – and The Twist by a man named Chubby. She said that anybody who's been to church feels how music moves the hearts and souls of people. So, I got my record player and put on* *all my Elvis 45s. She likes Elvis, too. My heart - and soul got quite a workout! Sophie*

Sophie *– today - Laura at school told me her father would give her $100 when she graduates high school to go to a nearby trade school or get married. She works a few hours a week as a waitress at Hunters Restaurant. There, she receives a pocket change from the discarded nickels, dimes, and pennies and a rare quarter left on a dirty table. With $100, she could buy a car and leave town until the car broke down at nowhere with nothing and no one. So why do her brothers get to go to college? Why is she worth less, and why does she accept this without question? And then yesterday, her father took her kitten to the city dump and left it there because it scratched him.*

And then, Alice, in my math class – her mother was taken to the hospital after she would not wake up. She died. The bottle of pills she took for her headaches was empty. Alice now stays home to care for her 2-year-old sister and walk her 7-year-old brother to school. What happens to her dreams of being an airline stewardess?

Why are girls at the mercy of some mythical prince suddenly appearing and choosing us? *Does anyone care about what I want – or do not want? Here is a clue: secretary, teacher, house cleaner, hairdresser, beautician, or waitress are not on my list. I guess becoming the president option is a previously determined no-chance situation as well. Who made these rules? Tell June Cleaver that cookies and milk* *will not convince me that peaceful monotony is a life worth living.*

I asked Miss Ellie the other day how much I should worry about my future. She said she is too busy getting through the day to worry about what tomorrow will bring. Life keeps you too busy to notice the passage of time.

If I knew or had some clue about what lies ahead, it would help me make better decisions today.

WILDFLOWERS FOR MISS ELLIE

Sophie *– Monday, August 21, 1961. I got very horrible, sad news. Miss Ellie. She just died. Went to sleep and never reappeared. No warning. No goodbye. No final hug. Just gone. Her neighbor called to tell me early this morning. I am trying hard to dress and go to her home and her people. But the whole world's weight is pushing me to the floor. So, I have no mother, sister, aunts, uncles or cousins, grandparents, and now, no Miss Ellie. I do have a father who barely acknowledges me**. I feel like the last butterfly in the garden at the end of the season.** To die alone without notice and fall among the dead dogwood flowers.*

Plants don't die so much like people. Wildflowers and tomatoes don't do just fine and then go to sleep and never wake up the next day like Miss Ellie. And plants never leave other dead flowers at the doorstep or threaten other plants with burning crosses. Nor do plants often get pushed downstairs or have the mark of the devil. They don't get pneumonia. Petunias don't die suddenly, without notice, and alone. No, plants die slowly from human neglect and lack of love and attention. Like people living in misery in that regard – only people are better at hiding the anguish. Where people expire without advance notice – plants let you see when they need attention to continue.

In an instant, Miss Ellie was gone. No notice. No hug. Happy memories of her have become the most painful and precious.

***Sophie** – Tuesday, August 22, 1961. I awoke this morning, and from my second-story window, the world outside disappeared into a cloud. I felt like Rapunzel in a tower - safe, secure, and lonely. Just me - waiting for my Prince Charming to arrive. Within minutes, the fog retreated to allow reality to seep into view as I heard father trip over something downstairs and mutter unmentionable words. Fact vs. fairy tale -- it is hardly a fair fight. Gee, I wonder how long before others miss me at school. I don't want to tell anyone there about Miss Ellie's passing. My "friends" will act as if they care and then ask each other, "Why does she care?" I can't handle that for the time being. They can do without me for a bit and marvel at my silence. Today, I just fell into a bottomless black hole. Within the gentle breeze, I watched the fallen leaves chase each other and dance in a circle on the driveway. Suddenly, it is all so pointless.*

Life is proof that fairy tales are merely propaganda.

I took the lilac dress Miss Ellie kept at my house to Maybell. She is the one in charge of the service and a good friend of Miss Ellie's. Miss Ellie wore that dress to Maybell's wedding. (Gee, I wonder how Louis will now steal from her and beat her up.) Maybell and I hugged and cried.

***Sophie** – Friday, August 25, 1961, at the funeral service for Miss Ellie at her church in nearby Lake*

Helen. Where the pine trees stretch to touch the clouds.

One by one, people stood and spoke of her greatness. She was a Friend, the closest I have to a real Sister, a Helper, like a Mother, the best neighbor, a great Friend, a churchgoer, and more.

Finally, I stood before the group and added: "Miss Ellie was present nearly every day of my life since my mother died when I was young. She showed up to each of my "not so great" recitals and birthday parties as I grew up. She taught me to dance to Chubby Checker music, lose at card games, do needlepoint, make the world's best fried chicken and sugar cookies, and love everyone – no matter what.

"She told me how proud and how much she loved each of you as you graduated from kindergarten or got to high school, when Elsa Mae started walking when Miss Bessie was in the parade with the children she cares for, and when members of this church took Thanksgiving dinners to the homes of so many grateful people. She told me how much she loved her church and the people here today. And she prayed for others every day – often multiple times a day.

"She talked about her church and community family and how that is the greatest gift anyone could have. She was more than a friend to me. She was my mentor, my guardian, and my role model in life. She was my

Fairy God Mother with whom I shared my hopes and dreams.

"Finally, I want to share some beautiful words Miss Ellie taught me. Miss Ellie was a mountain of wisdom whose words will live on forever. I still talk with her and can hear her talking to me. For example, she told me:

- *See happy and good to be happy and good.*

- *There is much more to see without your eyes.*

- *Hate steals your love for and from others.*

- ***The greatest gifts from God – are rainbows, wildflowers, and you.***

- *It is the grandmothers and great-grandmothers who are changing the world today. They make it possible for young mothers to get a job and go to work – and one day, send their daughters to college.*

- *There is always a way to make today better for someone.*

- *Pack up your mistakes and fling them into the heavens. They become a star and show the world that we all make mistakes. Mistakes guide us.*

- *She said, "You keep the love you share with others."*

I owe my most humble and sincere gratitude to each of you for sharing this remarkable lady with me. I miss her so very, very much."

I stepped down and hugged those I knew as others sat in the pews with their heads down as tears silently fell into their lap. I looked over those in attendance. So, this is love, I thought. Her family and friends, her community of care, the contributions that create love, and her unrelenting care for others above herself. She is the closest example I can feel of a loving family. One that I can only truly appreciate in the pain of death. I placed her favorite wildflowers upon her grave that day before going to what now feels to be the other end of the spectrum, that being home, to cook dinner for an ungrateful father.

Several invited me into their homes for some food, but I stayed at the cemetery after all others had left. There was something wrong about leaving her alone. Miss Ellie was always alongside me. She and I played with dolls and dressed up; she read me books about magical life and told me a best friend is the greatest gift God provides. She introduced me to the reflection of my sister. She told me that life was a challenge and equal parts wonder and difficulty. And how death was easy. She provided a bond of life beyond this time and place.

Sophie *– Saturday, August 26, 1961. There was no sunshine or singing birds at the cemetery this morning. All were defeated by the dismal grey sky holding the* *morning hostage. What now, Miss Ellie?* ***Where is the Prince and happily ever after I was promised?***

What gives death the right to repossess all wisdom, love, and kindness?

Miss Ellie, please tell me how to put all faith and love into a God who can stop the pain but chooses not to*.*

It is the perfect storm within the mayhem. All humanity has fled. Yet my soul is full of echoes – as if someone is calling me home.

Sophie *–Thursday, August 31, 1961. I did not return to school until yesterday. No one asked. I did not offer any reason for my absence. It was as if they each knew to give me time and space. After class, I asked teachers what I would need to do to make up my work. Each told me not to worry about it. How can I help but feel everyone knows my business better than I do? Do they realize I sat and cried before my mirror for days?*

Sophie *– Saturday, September 2, 1961. Maybell tells me Miss Ellie's Father was killed in a construction accident when she was about 4. Her mother brought her by train to Lake Helen from Georgia soon after to pick oranges. Her mother passed away a few weeks after they arrived - from an infection. Miss Ellie was looked after and raised by others in the community. That same community had taken up donations and ordered a headstone for her.*

Today, the morning drive to the cemetery was a quiet one of soft, gentle sunshine. I sat on the ground and started crying. What now, Miss Ellie? Death is the most profound cruelty in both the infinite and the moment.

Death is rude. It does not ask permission. It simply reaches down and turns off the light. At what point does death become a comfort, and is that just transferring the pain to the living?

I am unsure of the connection, but I suddenly realized how much I intensely hated my father. After suppressing it for years, it was as if a revelation and relief exploded in my head. His miserable existence is an annoyance, outrageous embarrassment to my friends, a concern as to what he would do next or what I was to do if he got sick or worse – and to whom could I turn for help.

Where Miss Ellie had a large extended family, I have everything but that. The food shopping, cooking, cleaning, laundry, and more than father demands - yet does not help, thank, or do anything to make anything easier. He does not even know my damn name.

Miss Ellie told me that life for women is about making sacrifices today to make tomorrow better for someone else. Women have always cleaned up the damage men make. Women are the ones who keep the family peace and organize the mayhem. It may be time women run the world in a civilized manner. I want a tee shirt that says, ***"June Cleaver is not my role model."***

Cindy – June Cleaver was the doting, pearl necklace, dress-wearing, stay-at-home mother of Beaver and Wally Cleaver, and the dedicated wife of Ward. *"Leave It to Beaver"* was a popular TV show from 1957-1963 that portrayed the idealized family life of the time.

*****Sophie*** *– Sunday, September 3, 1961. Perhaps Time is the Devil. It is a menace even God seemingly cannot control. As the Divine gently convinces wildflowers to paint a distant meadow in majestic shades of purple, Time haphazardly launches a random thunderbolt to scorch the same earth. Love may be all you need, but ultimately, some underappreciated measure of time is all you are given. Nothing makes sense. Miss Ellie says, "Miss Sophie, follow your heart, but always remember to stay safe."*
Sophie *-Thursday, September 14, 1961. Tonight, a black blanket draped over the streetlights throughout*

the town and snubbed out the wonder and light of stars. Crickets huddled silently beneath the bushes. Cars were motionless. The view from my window was only shades of dark, smothering all signs and sounds of life.

Where can I put the insecurities and fear within my soul and away from the light of day? ***I want off this planet before I hate everyone...***

Last night, I dreamed of Miss Ellie and me sitting in the countryside filled with wildflowers and blowing dandelions into the heavens.

Sophie *- Saturday, October 7, 1961. Miss Judy, the bank teller from downtown, was downstairs making father breakfast this morning – as she has lately done on Saturdays since Miss Ellie passed. I woke up last night and saw her car in the driveway. I suppose father does have a few friends – even if this one is young and pretty. She cooks a few meals and places them in the refrigerator, takes father's suits to the dry cleaner, and does general cleanup in the house and grocery shopping. I do the laundry, daily dishes, and change sheets. She is pleasant, and I try to help. She comes here twice a week.*

Sophie *– Friday, October 13, 1961. Miss Ellie had started putting father's clean clothes downstairs about June of this year. She told me once that she was happy he was staying downstairs because he kept a gun and bullets in the top bureau drawer in his upstairs* *bedroom. She saw it when putting away his laundry long ago.*

He had been mainly staying downstairs. His recliner was there when he watched TV, his desk and files, and the phone for doing some work at home. He usually slept on the sofa – I put a sheet and blankets on him, along with his favorite pillow. I maintained that setup for him.

Sophie *– Saturday, October 14, 1961. Fall time at the Boulevard Drive-In. Now that it is cooler, Melody and her family asked to take me to the Drive-In (also known as the DeLand Passion Pit). In the last few months, we have seen Oceans 11, West Side Story, and Dr. No – a James Bond movie. But I refused to see Psycho. No, thanks. A few pesky mosquitoes still refuse to give in to the cooler weather and make themselves a nuisance, but it is still fun. I see many school guys there showing off their treasured wheels. At school on Friday, Sue told me she and Roger are considering running away right after graduation to avoid his draft to Vietnam. Already, his uncle was killed there.*

Cindy – The Boulevard Drive-In on Woodland Boulevard south of town. The drive-in movie opened in 1954, and about 400 cars of people enjoyed outdoor movies until the outdoor screen was seriously damaged in a storm. The Drive-In closed in 1993.

Sophie – *Sunday, October 15, 1961. Autumn leaves are dancing outside my bedroom window this morning. It was a spontaneous grand finale performance of playful beauty – before succumbing into compost below. The birds were welcoming the first streams of light peeking through the trees with an awkwardly broken melody of happiness – I think! I remember the early, gentle autumn days when I slept late as a child and lingered in bed with Miss Ellie at my side. I was terrified of a monster waiting to push me down the stairs. She promised to keep me safe – and did that very well as millions of leaves sacrificed themselves to try to bury this house from the light of day.*

Sophie – *Today – whatever it is. Some girls and I went and visited an Old Age Home nearby. Women of wealthy families whose possessions are reduced to a bed and some meager contents on a single dresser cabinet. The control of their world and possessions was down to their arm's length and ability to grasp. Some are simply heaps of crumpled indignity and full of missing memories. They were starved for attention and waiting patiently to die. We tried to cheer them up a bit. Some appreciated it – some just scowled.*

Sophie – *Tuesday, October 24, 1961. Measures of time - it was an assignment to define some ways to measure time. As I wrote it, the thought became clearer and simultaneously more remote. I include part of it here because Mr. Tromley read it out loud to the class and asked Mrs. Henries to include it with the Princeton University scholarship application.*

I was feeling incredibly alone the evening I wrote it. Some examples of time I included migrations, phases of the Moon, carbon dating, germination, and generations. Time is perhaps the common element within all things, processes, systems, thoughts, and feelings in the universe.

Everything is either growing or decaying. Time is change – and change is time. It structures, restructures, and replaces all things - except perhaps Love. I called the paper "The Ever-changing Constant of NOW."

Some other examples of measures of time I recall providing include:

Old Faithful.

Equinox.

Solar and lunar eclipses.

The Big Bang.

Geo strata.

Photographs.

Metamorphosis.

And A Diary!

***The only unmeasurable units of time are the Present and Love, as each is unending and unchanged by any force in the universe.**

Sophie - *Thanksgiving – November 23, 1961. After a brief visit, Randal, my neighbor, and best friend is away again. He got to tell me a bit about how challenging college is – but he is determined to get through it. He works with a veterinarian on a horse ranch in his spare time.*

Sophie - *Saturday, December 16, 1961. A bunch of us went to watch the Christmas parade downtown. I loved the band! Then, off for some ice cream at Rodeo Whip and browsing through McCrory's and Department Stores for Christmas ideas. My favorite float was the one that said – "All we want for Christmas is Peace," and another called "Hatter Madness" with a big Stetson hat.*

Sophie – *Tuesday, December 19, 1961. Randal came home from college today. He is looking forward to becoming Dr. Peterson soon!*

Sophie – *Sunday, December 24, 1961. I spent it with my father in the Emergency room. He fell and cut his leg on the front door brick steps. They x-rayed it and stitched it up. He has crutches. They gave him pain medicine and special dressings I must change for him. He blamed me for making him fall. Miss Ellie's extended family brought over some turkey and mashed potatoes for father and me. I hugged them. I also made pies and chocolate chip cookies for them (and Mrs. Williston). Once they left, I closed myself in my room and cried.*

HER NAME WILL BE WINSLOW

Events in 1962:

- *"Stranger on the Shore"* by Acker Bilk becomes a hit.

- February 20, 1962, John Glenn became the first American to orbit Earth in Friendship 7.

- April 9, 1962, *West Side Story* won the Academy Award for Best Movie.

- April 21, 1962, the World's Fair opened in Seattle, Washington.

- May 24, 1962, Scott Carpenter orbits Earth in Aurora 7.

- July 2, 1962, the first Walmart opened in Rogers, Arkansas.

- August 5, 1962, Actress Marilyn Monroe died of an overdose.

- September 23, *The Jetsons*, an animated program, premiers on TV.

- October 14, the Cuban Missile Crisis began.

Cindy - While 1962 is the shortest time she spent with her diary (6 months, it contains some of the longest posts. The pages indicate she had found her writing style and thoughtful passion.

Sophie – *Monday, January 1, 1962! Welcome, 1962! My favorite music is anything on Dick Clark's American Bandstand! Mr. Kennedy is about to become President. The world is getting so busy at the same time my life is! S*

Sophie -*Thursday, January 4, 1962. Today is Randal's birthday! He is 21 years old. I sent him a card last week and some homemade chocolate chip cookies he likes. He is about to start going to Veterinarian school. I am not sure where that will be. But he has all the plans in place to go.*

Sophie – *Friday, January 19, 1962. I figured out the best way to communicate with father on Friday evenings (and mitigate the most mess) is by concealing a well- padded couch (spreading out newspapers helps) with a blanket, pillow, and a nearby trash can. I moved away furniture to allow extra room should he wish to attempt to get to the bathroom without further crash landings.*

Sophie - *January – sometime. Christmas should be extended two weeks longer, and February should start two weeks earlier. OK, maybe that won't help the plants and animals, but it would make me feel better. January is just a miserable excuse for a month. Some plants are skeletons, and others hide from the cold. There is brittle abuse in frigid dirt. I hate January. Bears have the right idea with hibernation. Just sleep through it -*

there is nothing for them to hear or do other than dream of Spring.

But wait – there is more!

January is a pathetic follow-up to the joy of December and a disappointment to start the promise of a new year with such a dismal and depressing month. The sky is heavy and sad. The flowers hide beneath the dirt while the squirrels run among the gray shadows and search for food, and the birds, along with any hope, have fled further south to find some sun. At least February has some promise of March. January has nothing to brag about; it is just to endure. I feel so much better when I have something to dislike and blame all the world's ills upon.

Sophie *– Saturday, February 3, 1962. Randal's nephew, Antonio Peterson, is one year old today! He went directly from walking to running on the same day and never seemed to stop! I enjoy babysitting for him and playing. He is so much fun! I send pictures of him to Randal when he is away at school. I went to his birthday party after school today and got him a pull-around turtle. SS*

Sophie *– Friday, February 16, 1962. father said he must calm the torments with his spirit bottle of "remedy." Miss Ellie once said it much more eloquently and told me he was just drunk. He works during the week and comes home late every other Friday evening from a board meeting – so he says. I set up things to* *encourage him to sleep downstairs on the couch. I give him breakfast and coffee on Sunday mornings before church.*

There was a disagreement with his accountant, and father came home late tonight and was angry. Miss Ellie told me once that he fights with inner demons. I think she is right – as always.

Miss Ellie once said, "People have different amounts of strong and fragile. Your father, Mr. Sherman, has a lot of fragile. You, you have mountains of strength. And where he insists on respect – even though he is a powerful man, you earn your respect daily on how you treat and help others. Miss Sophie, you are a wonderful young lady – don't let Mr. Sherman make you think otherwise."

Sophie *– Tuesday, February 20, 1962. John Glenn orbits the Earth. I am so jealous! I bet Sierra is, too!*

Sophie *– Friday, March 9, 1962. Happy birthday to my number 15! Randal was home and gave me the cutest, most energetic little white puppy. She is just adorable in every way. I named her Winslow - the name I like and want to call my daughter someday. After a party with his family at his house, Randal returned to college. He said he also enjoyed going to the beach with Antonio.*

Cindy – As Jonathan had previously told me, a dog was given my name before I was born! I also suspected my name was intended to be Winslow Sherman. It would explain the "WS" for Winslow Sherman on the small towel Mother had likely hand embroidered. That towel was brought with me (as a newborn infant) along with a "tattered rag doll" to the Emergency Room when Sophie fell down the stairs, hit her head, and passed away on March 30, 1963. Those two items were likely mailed to Walters along with Sophie's Death Certificate, Coroner Report, and my Birth Certificate. They were probably added to his backyard bonfire.

Here is the photo again of my Mother. I look at it often, hoping she feels my adoration for and of her. Both Sophie and Winslow appear to be waiting patiently for me.

https://pixabay.com/photos/puppy-young-lady-kiss-kisses-2681767/

Image by JackieLou DL from Pixabay

Sophie - Monday, March 12, 1962. Puppy dogs are such fabulous creatures. You readily know when they are happy.

Dogs want to be your best friend. I have set up things to keep her in my bedroom while I am at school. I have her toys, water, food, some puppy pads I made for her, and a way for her to hop up on my bed. I moved away anything she should not chew on and other breakable things out of her reach. We go for a walk as soon as I get home. She loves it.

*I never knew such joy before Winslow came into my life. Sometimes, I think Miss Ellie returned in this form to help watch over me. **If you are a really good person, you are reincarnated as a happy puppy!** Miss Ellie once said cats are poetry and grace until another cat enters their territory. But dogs, dogs are happy and want to be your best friend. Dogs are love and companions no matter what. Sophie*

***Sophie** – Saturday, March 17, 1962. An unusual amount of total calm and quiet awoke me this Spring morning. The birds were silent and hiding. Squirrels refused to scurry about the yard and in sight of my second-story bedroom window. The breeze had suddenly dropped to the ground to protect the insects below from impending doom. And in the opposite, but hardly equal measure, approaching from the east was the low booming of enormous kettle drums threatening to shatter the silence as Mother Nature prepared to* *dump out her legends of wash water from the heavens and onto us below.*

I gently awoke Winslow, who was snuggly asleep beside me. I quickly took her out into the backyard for her morning duty as a scattering of the first few large raindrops splatted on the porch decking as a final warning to the wise. Thankfully, she was not interested in taking her time, so we returned inside and quickly closed the windows. Sophie

Sophie *– Sunday, March 18, 1962. The chirping Cardinals at the front yard birdfeeders woke me up this morning. Thank God for Springtime! Winslow and I run around the yard chasing each other, trying to fly with the butterflies and scattering piles of fallen leaves in all directions.*

I recall Miss Ellie once saying I am too young to be so old – right now, I am too old to feel so young. Winslow is a joy. She is a wonderful puppy who makes me laugh at simple things and feel joy and love. Miss Ellie would have loved her, too.

She has become my soul mate, and we share a joy beyond friendship. We create happiness and comfort in the company of others. It helped me to see how teenage friends are so self-centered. Each statement starts with "I" – each thought concerns themself only. Whereas a dog forgives and listens. Dogs are spiritual animals. ***I am the dreamer; Miss Ellie is the wisdom;***

*and **Winslow is just joy.** May everyone have all three in equal measure each day.*

Winslow licks my face in the morning before any rude alarm clock interrupts my dreams. She makes me smile when I am lonely. She is quiet when I want to be alone and my best friend when I need one.

***The best people return as the best and happiest puppies.** It is the only thing to explain the bond and the dedication. The best Angels may be trained in Hell, but caring people get to return as best lifelong canine friends to remind us that joy can be found anywhere at any time.*

Cindy - At 15, she had become quite an independent young lady, further determining her future in women's liberation.

***Sophie** – Friday, April 6, 1962. Women can care for themselves, make wise decisions, care for others - and run businesses, organize, operationalize, create, and accomplish anything – if men would just quit insisting otherwise. Men need us so much more than we need them.*

The age of women is coming. We are more intelligent, kinder, and more resilient. Men's "superior leadership" has burdened the country with wars and oppressed people. It is time for men to spend much of their lives cooking and cleaning.

*I so need Miss Ellie to help me be strong. **How do***

you measure or contain the depth and dimension of love and determination? How will I get through without her?

Cindy - And some of Sophie's entries were quite long....

Sophie - *Early Saturday, April 7, 1962. Winslow helped herself to the petunia bed of Mrs. Williston next door yesterday. She freely arranged the helpless flowers and liberated ample dirt in all directions. So, I walked my old red wagon downtown last evening to fetch a dozen new plants and potting soil from the Hardware Shop. Then, early this morning, I tied Winslow to a nearby tree and allowed her to watch me as I cleaned up for misbehavior before Mrs. Williston awoke. This must be like raising a child. You can't fire them, such as an employee, eject them from an organization, or ex-communicate them from church – you can only have patience, hope, and, in this case, a good trowel.*

Mrs. Williston has been a widow for a long time. It was as if she had found an unusual comfort in her sequestered misery. She would bang on the windows inside the home to scare the squirrels stealing bits of bird food from the feeders. She would grumble and verbally berate the dandelions she yanked from her yard.

Once, she told me of the many recipes she had memorized, but her ability to recall them was playing games of hide and seek. She attributed it to a mischievous child taunting her daily by hiding pieces of herself. Names are erased. Answers go blank. She was disappearing piece by piece.

She has lived alone with "Sinatra" for years after her husband's wartime death. She is a bit unsteady and slow and usually uses a cane. One day, she brought me into her home to pick up some homemade sugar cookies for me as a thank-you for the little things we did to help. Her house is cluttered with long-established knick-knacks that once, no doubt, brought joy. Today, they provide comfort with the familiar and act as stoic sentries, standing guard and protecting her memories and dusty, faded photographs of people who remain eternally youthful. The once sharp edges in her face had softened into gentle folds. She was kinder and more tolerant of what had previously annoyed her.

She was born in 1899 and impressed me as someone who just woke up "old" and wrinkled one day. It was something she could not get comfortable with, and as if time had erased the finer points of joy. But if you could get her to forget that she was interesting. I looked forward to our walks and talks when she told me about her adventures. It made me want to be elegant and thankful when I was old.

While walking to church one morning, she told me how she and her husband hoped to travel the world together – but an angry world had other ideas. They had some money and hoped to adopt some international children to help promote world peace. Her husband survived the battle in WWI only to become one of the earliest casualties while in Europe on business during the onset of WWII. She was a nurse, and he was a land developer for manufacturing plants.

"Every night before going to bed, he would look in each closet and under each bed, table, and couch for "jerries" as he called them. He thought there were still Germans waiting to kill us. I would even help him look to help calm him. Wars hurt everyone," she said. ***She told me that no one wins a war – you find a way to survive with what and who is left.***

"We would work hard and enjoy our golden years comfortably together. I did not count on losing him so soon or losing so much of myself. It is unfair to struggle to see a smile, hear the birds sing, or stroll carefree through a garden. I am so grateful for the kindness of young people such as yourself. It gives me hope that the world will become a better place."

"I enjoy this and am glad to help!" I said. Her skin stretched tight over her widened finger joints as she hung onto her cane.

"Yes, I am glad to be alive," she said. "And I feel some joy in each day. Thank you, Sophie – you are so very special to me."

Although Mrs. Williston does have a car and does drive to the stores, I told her I would drive her to church or other places if she wished. Today, she was talkative and wanted to walk and talk on a peaceful morning in her proper dress and a single strand of pearls.

Over the months, her memories and world seemed to evaporate in random amounts – as did her height and smile. She appeared to be living with a growing silence within her head.

Sophie *– Tuesday, April 10, 1962. Sierra does not want to get enamored with one guy and sail into blissful oblivion. I can't blame her, but that is the expectation for girls. Look at nearby role models. For example, Miss Ellie had a man who took her money and beat her. Mrs. Williston, next door, was left an unhappy and lonely old widow when her husband was killed in World War II. Mrs. Werther left high school to marry her sweetheart, and at age 22, she has two children and barely enough resources to feed herself. I have never seen her smile. And closer to home, my mother married a wealthy but abusive alcoholic.*

This is more in common with a parasitic existence than a prescription for enjoying life. Why is it assumed we can have no life without a man? Sierra likes her independence and making a difference for others. She has no regrets and no dependence upon a man to guide her life.

True passion goes beyond tempting short-term anecdotes of fairytales. I wish we could read the book of life ahead of the present. I hope someone would point to a realistic path and provide a clue of what lies ahead and how to get there. How do you be brave enough to follow your path? I want to be like Sierra - independent, help others, free of needing men, and make a difference. Randal's dad, Dr. Peterson, once told me, **"How you manage life from 15 to 25 years of age will determine how life will manage you."** *I think he is very correct!*

Cindy – And her philosophical bent continued...

Sophie *- Sunday, April 15, 1962. The Pastor said Jesus could be a poor, downtrodden man on a park bench. If that is true, I wondered if Jesus could also be a young colored girl crying as others kicked sand at her and called her names. Could Jesus be the wind through the trees? If so, then why is Jesus so elusive? I want to meet this guy and ask why there are selfish, judgmental, intolerant people – where is the good in that? Is conflict a requirement in this world to provide*

headlines for newspapers?

(A pencil drawing of a Monarch butterfly was also on the page.)

Cindy – Sophie had some unique insights and brave perspectives.

***Sophie** – April Thursday, April 19, 1962. **Where is the line dividing art from logic or between the breeze and the air?** Can one exist without the other, or do both contribute to the entire soul and spirit that makes life go forward and provide its purpose? A Ying requires a Yang. A Portrait requires a Person. A goal requires a purpose. There is so much more beyond the obvious. Ss*

***Sophie** – Saturday, April 21, 1962. From Winslow the dog - Trix I tot my human to do! I showed Sofy how to climb a tree. So, she did 2. But she fell into the pile of leaves. It was a lot of fun. I did, too. Winslow*

Okay, so I taught my puppy how to write - badly. Sophie PS – We did have fun!

I put pictures of her in my closet, with my yearbooks, old school papers, newspapers, and photographs of friends and Randal, Miss Ellie, Christmas, birthday cards, and the parade mementos. I am trying to figure out why I should save some of these except to keep memories of people and places I always want to remember. It shows the world we were here, even if I question whether anyone cares about the soon-gone reality of old pictures. A bit weird.

Cindy - So many diary entries demonstrated the youthful exuberance in the 1960s. She mentions the local music band flyers, movie ads, pictures, ice cream receipts, ticket stubs, and dried flowers she placed in a box on her bedroom closet shelf. So much of the evidence of her life and times vanishes amid the Florida breeze and smoke in early 1964.

***Sophie** – Monday, April 23, 1962. I got the scholarship letter from Princeton University!!! Mrs. Henries gave it to me today in school. She had it framed for me. So, when I graduate high school with at least a B average, my entire four-year degree in Natural Sciences from Princeton will be paid! I am glad. I gave Mrs. Henries a huge hug. I showed it to father. He said, "Girls don't need to go to college," and walked away. I quietly took one of his framed pictures off the wall and put my scholarship letter within the same frame and on the same nail. I am anxious to show it to Randal!*

father never comments on anything I do other than make a loud racket on the piano. I wonder whether he considers me to be his daughter or just an ugly disappointment.

Cindy - And likewise, the turbulence and influence within the times she grew up did not escape her.

***Sophie** - Friday, May 3, 1962. Today in English class, Miss Meadows asked Janet to read her paper to* *the class about how she would improve the world. Janet read how she would plant more trees. Trees make homes for animals and provide shade and oxygen. Trees don't go to war. Trees don't fight. Trees don't hate. People kill trees to make roads and buildings for themselves. People go to war, and some don't come home. People hurt other people. Trees reach to touch the sky and make peaceful places. Majestic trees gracefully accept life with dignity. Too many people don't. Trees enjoy life. I want to be a tree to make the world a better place.*

We spent the rest of the class time talking about the Vietnam War. The class knew three people who had died there.

Sophie *– Sunday, May 5, 1962. I could do without reminders like the Doomsday Clock and everyone thinking another is out to kill them, so consequently, they plan to kill them first. How can I protect the Athens Theater and my church if someone wants to blow up Florida? I wonder if I could write to President Kennedy or some head guy in Russia.*

Everyone I see seems so angry and stressed. Why can't we have a contagious epidemic of tranquility? According to the news, everything on and circling the world is just a man-made mess programmed in destruct mode. Everyone seems to be the enemy – and I bet they think the same of us. Perhaps we all have something in common after all. Good and evil differ in more ways than just being opposite. Good is fleeting, monetary scraps of time in short bursts of endurance. *Evil has a lasting impact and lives on in memory as continuous bits of horror.* **Evil destroys for long periods, while good is the shimmer of hope hidden among the rubble.**

MY SISTER'S KEEPER

__Sophie__ – Monday, May 14, 1962. Miss Ellie once said that God watches from behind the mirror. father must have overheard that, and he took it seriously last night.

Tonight, father went around shooting all the mirrors in the home (except the one in my room) with his handgun. He said he did not like who he saw staring back at him. Despite avoiding the stairs for the past few months, he made it upstairs to get his gun from his top bedroom bureau drawer. He went around the house, yelling at the mirrors, and later, I heard him put his gun back in his bedroom bureau drawer before the police arrived. Miss Ellie told me he had a gun and bullets in it. She was right, and he had not forgotten about it.

The Police came. I guess the neighbors called. I was hiding in my bedroom and holding Winslow. My bedroom door was locked. father did not try to go in. The Police never found me, nor did they find his gun. It needs to be taken away from his bedroom. Miss Ellie told me it was where he kept his clean socks. I was surprised father made it up the stairs to his bedroom to get the gun. He has been sleeping downstairs for the past several months. And I heard him go back upstairs before the Police arrived – probably to put his gun back into its hiding place.

The Police were here for about an hour, looking for ideas as to why father would do this, looking for his gun, and looking for me. They did not find the gun or me despite me unlocking my bedroom door when they arrived to keep them from breaking it down. I hid in my closet with Winslow behind the posters, hanging clothes, and books I kept there.

Once things were quiet and I could hear him snoring downstairs, I looked into the vanity mirror and asked in a whisper if she was OK. She looked sad and worried and reached out her hand to touch mine.

While hiding in the closet, I created a plan for tomorrow after father goes to work.

Sophie *– Tuesday, May 15, 1962. She is not here, but I wanted to tell Miss Ellie I was afraid to go to school. People talk; they will have heard all about Dad last night. But if I don't go to school, they will talk more.*

Then I could hear what Miss Ellie would say in my head – "I know you can keep a secret. And you can't stop people from talking, but you can show them you don't care if they talk. Because you KNOW what happened and will not share that with them, please don't give them anything more to yammer about. Just walk away if you need to."

She provides sound advice – even if it is just imaginary. But today, I have a plan – and it requires I be home --- alone.

I will wait until father leaves today. I'll play Hooky from school. I would not let him think I was still home and had not already gone to school.

From my bedroom window, I watched as father drove away. I went into father's room and opened the top dresser drawer. I saw the gun – all the bullets were spent. More empty shells were scattered throughout the drawer and among old handkerchiefs and socks. There was also a heavy box mostly full of bullets. I left the handkerchiefs and socks and placed the remaining items in an empty box I had brought. I noticed beneath the now less compressed socks a pile of neatly folded papers that had otherwise been hidden from view. I had not seen or known of these before.

Within the papers was a postcard dated March 12, 1947. It said – Congratulations on your bonus blessings from God! The signature was too blurred to read. The card was addressed to Mrs. Camille Sherman. From the first view, among other documents, there appeared to be the Police and Ambulance papers regarding my mother on the day the ambulance came. There was a written quote on a form where she said, "I pushed her down into Hell. She has the mark of the devil." There were also two identical newborn dresses and two pairs of tiny matching pink shoes.

Visions and sounds of that day so long ago flashed in my head. I gathered up all the papers, gun, and ammo, intending to lock them and myself into my bedroom. I left the baby items beneath the socks to compensate for the previously occupied space. I tried to leave my father's drawer with the appearance of not being tampered with – in hopes his easily distracted short attention span would have no cause to notice the missing gun or anything out of place.

Once back in my room, my heart was racing. I was a bit dizzy and out of breath. I shut my door and locked it – despite realizing I was home alone.

First, a quick look at the gun showed it was empty of bullets, and I dumped out the empty shells.

I gently took apart the folded papers. They were documents of some kind... a neatly folded, undisturbed, and compressed pile of papers. There were five original documents:

*1. **Police report** of a disturbance on February 23, 1951, at the home of Walters Sherman on West Minnesota Ave, DeLand, Florida.*

*2. **Ambulance report** of an injured and deceased child at the bottom of stairs and a hysterical woman on February 23, 1951, at the home location.*

*3. **Birth Certificate** of Saufi Irene Sherman*

*4. **Birth Certificate** of Sharline Ivy Sherman*

*5. **Death Certificate** with **Coroner Report** of Sharline Sherman*

Memories invaded from all directions.

Sophie - *The original ambulance and police records were handwritten and legible. Mrs. Sherman (mother) is quoted as "I pushed her down into Hell" when asked what happened to her injured child at the bottom of the basement stairs.*

I still often wonder why people act as if I don't realize I have a sister. Why are they denying her existence and our collective pain?

I glanced again at the birth certificates. I do have a middle name! Our initials are both SIS. I had to wonder if that was intentional. We have a middle name because this piece of paper has a better memory than anyone. It is Irene! And Sophie is spelled differently! Saufi Irene Sherman! And Sharline Ivy Sherman! And then I saw what I already knew in Sharline's Coroner Report and Birth certificate.

Cindy - There were multiple entries in her diary on the same day – May 15, 1962.

I remembered the day. Mrs. Williston from next door came to see how she could help with the commotion. I remember sitting on the kitchen floor, holding my Sophie doll, and crying for my hurt sister. Mrs. Williston picked me up and took me away from the scene of my crumpled sister below on the basement floor. She held me and asked the name of the doll I was holding tightly. "Sophie," I said. Mrs. Williston has called me Sophie ever since. My sister held her Sharline doll and lay motionless at the bottom of the stairs. In the background, my mother was screaming about pushing my sister down the stairs because she had "the mark of the devil" over and over, and soon, the Ambulance came.

About that time, a Policeman came into the room with Mrs. Williston and me. He asked her questions and the child's name at the bottom of the stairs. I was afraid and started crying. Where was he taking my sister? Was he going to take me away, too? Mrs. Williston told the Police Officer that Sharline was at the bottom of the steps and my name was Sophie. Even then, I wondered if it was intentional in case my mother found out.

Cindy - Written in Sophie's diary on the same day:

Memories flooded my brain. We had matching cloth dolls with brown yarn hair wearing blue dresses and bloomers – but we could tell them apart because one had a spot on her leg – under her bloomers. Once we were separated from sharing one large crib to sleeping in matching separate beds in the same room, we kept each other's doll to feel like we were still together. We were three years old (not quite four) then. Before words were needed, we shared silently between our intertwined souls.

Mrs. Williston stayed with me until another lady showed up later. It was Miss Ellie. Miss Ellie slept in the matching bed in my room upstairs – or in the same bed with me when I was afraid someone would push me down the stairs. Then, finally, she moved into the guest room when I was about six years old. She called me Sophie.

These paper documents had been hidden for so long and forgotten by many – including, hopefully, father. He would be furious and perhaps violent if he knew I had these documents. He had gone out of his way to keep this from others. I must make plans to leave here beyond father's grasp. College. That will get me out of here – safely and carefully. It is time to take charge of my NOW, starting here.

*I don't see it as a lie but as protecting a sacred secret. There had been no proof until I found this evidence today. **My world and life had become comfortable in the convenient distortion of facts that gullible others chose to believe. It was the best I could do within the limitations of being permitted but one life at a time and wishing to keep my sister at my side – and my father from potentially killing me.***

So, what do I do with it? I can't just burn the proof of my sister (and consequentially, myself) in the fireplace.

But perhaps, maybe I SHOULD! Or I could find a safe place to put the evidence (and this diary) - away from here. Some places will remain undisturbed or undiscovered until I can safely pursue and investigate them later. I can't ask father about these papers – he might get angry. But I need a plan. I read about a *school in Arkansas. They provide room and board in exchange for working there. Princeton is not quite ready for me yet – and I would need father to sign a release. Then he could find me. We must be anonymous without leaving a trace of where we go. I will be in 10th grade soon.*

And .... One time, Miss Ellie told me that the truth may set you free, but it seldom makes you happy. mother intended to kill me, and I recall father once threatened to throw my sister's doll into a raging fire, saying she cried too much. What would have happened without Miss Ellie?

The misdirection weighs heavy on my soul as reality is in plain sight.

*I long for the days before **I realized that happiness does not appear to live well alongside reality.** At the same time, happiness exists in the fleeting moments of charm, while the truth stains for all eternity.*

Where is my Fairy Godmother? And where do I park the guilt?

After finding the birth certificates and more, I awoke this morning with doubts, questions, and worry about life without Miss Ellie – but with only father. The bird did not help this from the tree outside my bedroom window, and its repeated three-word refrain of "cheater, cheater, cheater" ... Pause and repeat to taunt me...over and over.

I need a plan for the documents. Where do I put them for safekeeping, and who (if anyone) needs them? I need to get away for a bit and clear my head. Thankfully, Melody asked me to go with her to visit Cassadaga in a few days.

Cindy – Wow. What a load of information, fear, and insight! It is a lot to process. I took a break from reading the diary for a few days. I needed to think and unravel a story of deception, wisdom, terror, self-preservation, and survival. Is Sophie really Sophie? I must consider this further. Maybe a LOT further.

Cindy - Cassadaga is a small unincorporated community adjacent to Lake Helen and a few miles from DeLand. In 1894, the area became the Southern Cassadaga Spiritualist Camp. Today, it is a tax-exempt church and community that believes in a continuous life. Mediums are available to contact and communicate with those who have passed on. There is also a church, bookstore, classes, tours, speakers, Healers, and workshops.

B. Duffy

Sophie *– Saturday, May 26, 1962. Visit Cassadaga! "It's time to get away from DeLand (or Duh-land or Dull-land as Melody calls it!) Melody rode with me. Her middle name is Charm – I love it! Her parents are from Ireland, and she has a pile of shoulder-length curly red hair that the wind insisted on rearranging, and by her own admission, she is "absolutely infested with freckles!" She has a caged canary near the kitchen window named "Tweets." Seeing your freedom but not being permitted to touch it seems cruel. I felt sorry for the bird. Escape would be so liberating! Being locked in the most glorious castle ever is still a prison.*

Cassadaga is a quaint town with a small lake, unusual hills, and polite folk of uncommon skills. Melody talked me into making the trek with her. I figured why not – maybe some magic Medium mojo that I do not quite believe in could mend the rift separated by time and space – and perhaps help father to drive straight.

Melody is a happy person with a penchant for "liberating" various small cosmetics from McCrory's from time to time. But she also has a refreshing and surprising mindset of reasonableness – where bras are for comfort and not "display purposes" that I often see today. She is comfortable anywhere and adjusts readily to any situation. Despite her less flamboyant view on fashion, she wants to be a dancer on Bob Hope tours.

I drove my car and her to the Cassadaga Spiritualist Camp. Initially, the Medium I met was a bit freaky but kind and gentle. Her name was Deja – and soon, I felt comfortable as she gently held my hand.

I will try to recite the experience as it happened below:

"Sophie, you are going to make a lasting change in the world for decades to come," the black-haired, long pink fingernailed Deja said.

Ooohhh Kaaaay, I thought. Then I asked – "How?"

The Medium lifted her chin, closed her eyes, and said, "Wait! Camille. Your mother is here. She says she recognizes who you are. And she muttered something about a .... demon or devil mark? (OK – now, I am terrified). Does that make any sense to you? She is also asking for your forgiveness. But – wait – there is another." She paused and swung her long, curly red hair back as she never lost contact with my hand.

"There is a young lady. Related to you. She is --- your sister?"

WHAT? All right, obviously, she has done her homework. Let's play along, I thought. I was still so hoping this was legitimate, and said, "Yes, we are very close." I did not share further details. It was back when we shared thoughts. When words just got in the way. We could communicate without saying anything out loud.

Deja closed her eyes as she said, "Two souls sharing one image and reflection. There, you find both hope and love. She says all is well and she loves you very much -- but wants you to be careful. There is danger ahead." The lady said.

"You must tell me more," I insisted.

Her eyes were wide open as she said, "There is an encounter and then a trip ahead – you will travel. But you will not be entirely alone." She closed her eyes. "Also ...Winslow – her name will be Winslow. She will be searching for you. Make sure she gets your book."

"Winslow is my puppy. Perhaps she is lonely or hungry – I should get home to her," I said, a bit less unimpressed as my dog does not read books. But Miss Medium did not stop.

"There is so very much more. Your sister is distraught. Jonathan will be the messenger – go to him." she replied.

"My sister realizes I will always love her for all eternity. But now I am worried about my dog," I said. I was intrigued, but there was only so much altered timeline spiritual mojo that was too close to some form of reality that I could withstand. Next, she might tell me father wants to learn ballroom dancing and that I should join the circus. It's too late for that, I guess. The clowns have already infested my life.

She opened her eyes and let go of my hand. The connection to the cryptic beyond was broken. She acted as if she had provided fantastic information, which she had. Perhaps more than a bit creepy, though. Many people have heard stories and rumors about my mother and sister. Why would she be any different?

Nonetheless, I was uncomfortable. I apologized for leaving so soon and paid and thanked her before leaving the room.

About ten minutes later, Melody asked me what I thought about meeting with the Mediums. "Even after over a decade, everyone within a 50-mile radius knows all about my family except me. We are a celebrity of madness. There went a few bucks we will never have back. Let's get some ice cream. At least that will be money well spent."

"Sophie – All I heard is that your mother went away when you were young," Melody said.

"Yes, true – if only that was all – and the world, and we could just get over it," I said.

Melody responded, "And why do you so often refer to yourself as "we" – ya got a mouse in your pocket?"

I had to think about that for a moment before responding. And then I said -

"When I get lonely, I talk to my reflection in the mirror. When I get a haircut, so does she; when I have a blemish – she has a matching one on the other side of her face. We grew up together alone in my bedroom. She is my soul mate – and we were best friends growing up.

"So - how did yours go? What did your Medium say to you?" I tried to change the subject away from one that does not do well with words.

Melody said, "Yeah, well, she told me to find my meaning by reading Shakespeare and learning to swim. And apparently, someone is waiting to meet me in New Hampshire. None of this is likely to happen at any point in my lifetime!

"Mine mentioned Jonathan – who the hell is Jonathan? Any idea?"

"Uh, no. But this deserves ice cream. Rocky Road or plain ole chocolate?" she responded."

"Oh, Rocky Road! I'm buying. But – first, we need to check on my dog," I said.

We stopped by the house quickly. My puppy was fine and had been snoozing on the couch. Thankfully, father was not home.

Cindy – And then there were moments of insight from above that blurred the line between reality and imagination...

Sophie – *Sunday, May 27, 1962. Another day extracts itself from each life uniformly, without bias, regard, or apology. The sound of crickets welcomed the evening air. The squeals of childhood joy settled into a quieting slumber, and strife evaporated into contentment. As the day became old and surrendered to the twilight, the fireflies danced through the air as if to hold onto the last bits of scattered sunlight.*

The evening settled comfortably around and about me; I felt weightless. I could see the street and car lights gently coming to life from my bedroom window. I thought I could almost see the last glimmer of the sunset upon the St. John's River. Timid stars bravely started to peak through the pastel sky as the sun slipped toward the western horizon, leaving a soft glow to mark its descending path. The town feels at peace. I recall Miss Ellie telling me that goodness and joy live in gentle times and places – and to go there when you need comfort.

Here, the seagulls stretch their wings to soar among wispy clouds as strife evaporates into contentment above - as mayhem, deceit, and lies grow beneath the rooflines. But, for the moment, my town was peaceful and serene. And for that moment, so was I. Sophie

Cindy – Then the random thoughts and concerns invade two days later but on the same diary page .... The line between Sophie, Sharline, and Sierra is fuzzy.

Sophie *––Tuesday, May 29, 1962. I am alone among a sea of intimidation. Some are afraid of my father, and others assume I am well attended to but still question otherwise. I owe my life, well-being, concern, and care to one lady others refused to acknowledge. People cannot see or accept my world.* ***I live in a castle of alligators. I am a stranger within a world blinded by the fear of fear.***

I am looking forward to Princeton. (With some creativity and embellishment, Princeton almost sounds like Prince Charming!) I keep that goal and salvation in mind daily. Things will be so much better there. No one will know us or the "troubles" we endured. We will be among others with similar goals and hopes for the future. Together, we can set a path away and forward – with no past or current battles and onto new and unexplored territory. New friends. New Places. No secrets. No hiding. No lies.

Sophie *- Wednesday, May 30, 1962. Perhaps my alter ego was born again and currently lives as Sierra Sommers to wonder what happens to the future of history when incorrect assumptions are sustained.*

Next on the list of goals and places to visit for Sierra Sommers:

Buy a Stetson hat (not challenging to do in this town!) and some culottes to wear when riding my horse.

Machu Picchu, Visit Africa,

Fly a plane,

And Scuba dive.

Cindy – In some places, Sophie muddled the line between wishful reality, pure imagination, and her fictional escape within and, at times, as Sierra Sommers.

Sophie *– Monday, June 11, 1962. School Summer Vacation. Today, Sierra is thinking again about what she wants to do as she rinses her hair beneath a gentle waterfall on an obscure island off Hawaii. She is learning to scuba dive and wants to take pictures of manatees in the Spring near DeLand.*

Closer to home, I want to take a hot air balloon ride, maybe skydive, and camp out under the stars. I would love to explore the caves in France, visit the Great Wall in China, wander through Venice, and sail the Bahamas with Prince Charming. Someday, I want to sponsor a young girl, maybe one in South America, and write a book. Sierra Sommers has trained me well to take on the world. SS

Sophie – *Friday, June 15, 1962. father fired his Accountant, Mr. O'Reilly, for "moving his money to a company called IBM." father thought that was a "dumb name for a company." father also said, "It is about time I get a job. Volunteer work is not good enough."*

I will look for jobs in the newspaper this weekend. I was still disturbed by a frightful nightmare last night. I dreamed I was alone in the woods, and wolves ran after me. They could run faster than I could. There was no place to go, no one to help me, and no one could hear me begging and screaming for help. Sophie, I so need you... I was crying in my sleep. Sha

Cindy - I had not previously seen her "signoff" on diary submissions as "Sha."

FROM THE OTHER SIDE OF THE MIRROR

Sophie – *Monday, June 25, 1962. I woke up this morning to RUN, Sophie! It was softly written among the dew and dust of the morning on the vanity mirror in my bedroom.*

Ahh, yes – a girl's summer track run practice was to be this evening, but it was canceled last night because the coach was ill. That works out well because before father fired him, Mr. O'Reilly sent money to my bank account with the intent to sign up for the summer education program at John B. Stetson University. I need to go to the bank this morning to withdraw that and some money I had saved for Winslow's shots and the Vet visit coming up on Wednesday. Since I no longer have routine money deposited by Mr. O'Reilly, I will close the account.

I'll walk to Stetson University in the late afternoon to research Princeton University and see what I can find about Ladybugs in the garden. Unfortunately, the High School library had nothing before summer break, and the university library is quiet on Mondays in the early evening. Besides, the Sampson Library has wonderful Captain chairs – not the rickety old wooden kitchen table variety found at the high school. And the Holler Fountain is just glorious this time of year. The sound and sight of the water have a magical ability to make all distractions and trouble disappear.

I thanked the mirror for the reminder anyway.

Cindy - The Holler Fountain was at the World's Fair in 1939 in New York City. In 1951, William Holler, Jr. and Earl Brown purchased it as a gift to William Holler, Sr., and moved it to Stetson University, where it remains today.

Holler Fountain. Stetson University. Original Watercolor by Diane Erickson 2023.
diane1erickson@gmail.com

Cindy – The following had no date but was likely written in her diary later that day.

What happened next could not compete with my worst nightmare.

I was walking home from the University library after researching info about Princeton University and how to best use ladybugs in my garden. Very few cars were on the road, so I decided to take the long way home and buy a Coca-Cola at a nearby store. It was a bit before 7:30 PM, and despite the tall trees, dimming summer sunshine lingered in the sky.

Suddenly, an older teenage boy approached out of nowhere and asked if I wanted to learn about college life. He pointed to a large oak tree across the street in a densely wooded area. I declined and resumed walking home when two other boys came from behind the tree. Despite my protest, the boys quickly dragged me into the woods, put me on the ground, blindfolded, and gagged me. My notes about Princeton and insects scattered in the breeze.

I was confused and scared as they pushed me and held my arms and legs. I screamed for help as they held a washcloth over my mouth and a handkerchief over my eyes. One held down my arms and covered my mouth as the other held my legs and removed my old saddle shoes that I was trying to kick them with. They tore my clothes, hurt me, and lay upon me repeatedly. I cried. I begged as I heard the boys cheering for each other in whispered voices. I asked them to stop. I tried my best to yell for help. I prayed for my life. I relinquished control to God and begged for his gracious mercy upon my abusers and myself as dogs barked in nearby fenced backyards, open building windows yielded the sounds of students practicing on tubas, others were cheering an impromptu soccer or football game, trucks rumbled through the town, crows squawked, and a racket of deafening noisy cicadas filled the air.

It felt like an endless eternity of helplessness. The pain continued until one boy said in a hushed voice, "We have to get back to Daytona." They then turned me over and left me face down in the dirt as they rapidly disappeared through the trees. I was exhausted, dazed, scared, and afraid to breathe.

As soon as I could gather my wits and see they were gone, I got up, grabbed my notes and shoes, and ran barefoot home as fast as I could, bleeding from various areas, only to get more abuse from father.

I tried to explain what had happened. He blamed the event on me and called me a slut, saying college boys would never do such a thing unless I were a prostitute. He grabbed my arm, twisted it, pulled my hair, and repeatedly hurt me. As Winslow came running to my defense, he kicked her across the room. She slammed against the piano and lay motionless. Finally, I could escape his grip, pick up my unconscious dog, and retreated to my room. I locked the door - and half wished I was brave enough and knew how to put the bullets into his gun. The tears would not stop. It is challenging enough to ignore the physical pain, but the emotional uproar screams within me like a frantic banshee on fire. Where is my Fairy Godmother? What would Miss Ellie do? If I screamed or called the Police, *father would only get angrier. **My only salvation is realizing that no one can hear or see what I am scheming...***

God, where are you? What did I ever do to deserve this?

I turned on some music before turning on the shower so I could cry while sitting on the floor without being heard and hoping that washing blood, dirt, more blood, and tears down the drain would take the rage and pain with it.

Why does real-life kidnap your dreams and hold them, hostage, to the brutality of reality?

Never have I simultaneously needed help from the world and so desperately wanted to leave it all behind. So, diary, I tell you something I shall tell no other - I will collect father's gun and a box of ammo. I will sell it to the pawn shop downtown tomorrow. Mr. Bill at the pawnshop sympathizes with my situation with father. I will go there early tomorrow morning. I am sure he will keep this secret, and father never goes to the pawnshop.

With that money and what I got from the bank today (neither Winslow will be going to the Vet nor me to summer classes), I will purchase a train ticket on the AC Line as far away as possible. I will get a job until I can get into Princeton University – although I am unsure how to graduate from High School. I will work as a nanny or teacher or clean homes at night and on weekends and go to the local high school during the day. I will get to college and become the person I wish to be. Miss Ellie once told me how important it is to make the best of NOW. It is the very best thing we can do. At this NOW, any place is a better place to be.

Dear God, please take care of my sister, Miss Ellie, and Winslow, and give them each a hug from me. I feel so alone and considerably less brave without them.

I hope Randal is still home at this late hour – if so, I am leaving this diary with him for safekeeping and hope I can resume it someday in happier times. I put the documents in it.

Cindy – OK – currently, I also have my fair share of personal rage! Welcome to the Sherman House of Horrors & Abusive Hospitality. It took me a few moments to calm down and refocus my attention. I wish to go back in time and be the friend my Mother needed.

Wait! ***Documents?*** I could barely read through blurred, teary eyes and a fair amount of rage. Wait. Documents? What documents? At a time like this, she could think rationally! So, I took a brief break to recover and think. Why did this happen to her? Who were those older boys? Why would Walters treat her like this? What documents? Where? I reluctantly read more, wondering what else to do, expect, or where to look. My hopes once again crumbled into dust and scattered among the wreckage of time as I turned the page and read the final page of words from my Mother.

Sophie - *God, what are you preparing me for? Why do you give me opportunity and hope and burden me with injustice and deception? How do I bury my past and start a new life?* ***Miss Ellie told me never to allow rage to eat my soul, but how can I grow flowers atop a landfill of secrets and deception?***

GOD, can you see me?

All the women in my life have left me – my Mother, Sister, Miss Ellie, and my beloved Winslow. Where do I go when all hope is gone and misconceptions have become a reality?

Locking myself in my car while it is running in our closed garage to stop the madness and pain is, admittedly, an option.

Late tonight, when father is asleep, I will bury my dog in my front yard beneath the Magnolia tree Miss Ellie and I planted on my 9th birthday. There, butterflies and wildflowers may watch over her. I will say goodbye to Randal if he is home. And goodbye to DeLand, a wonderful town of kind, generous people.

I take with me the name and spirit of my sister, the soul of Sierra Sommers, and the endless love of Miss Ellie and my beloved dog, Winslow. Love is an unspoken language that crosses all time and space and echoes throughout eternity.

I sat before my mirror and begged her to please be brave and allow me to leave. We reached out to touch hands as tears ran down her cheek and landed on the dresser top before me. We must be brave.

I asked Sierra what she would do. Adventurous as always, she said, "Hope lives forever. Chase the sunset into the dawn of a new day. Whatever you seek is out there if you don't allow challenges to get in the way."

I tell Sierra it is likely very challenging to arrive at dawn by chasing a sunset. She replied, "Impossible is merely a word." I am arguing with myself.

I live within one body connected to two spirits and an illusion to all.

This diary is dedicated to my sister, Miss Ellie, and Winslow – in the belief we will meet again.

PS – I wonder how long it takes for father to realize I am gone. I just discovered he apparently ran his car into the garage door sometime today and broke it into an enormous pile of bits. He is passed out on the couch with his favorite bottle of "Remedy." The insanity war is over. He wins. Follow your heart,

Sierra, Sophie, Sharline

PS - Once again – Dear God, please inform my mother I take with me the only things I truly love – the name and spirit of my sister. If the world wants to call me Sophie, I am honored to give that life essence. Out of the madness and into the unknown ahead to find the gentle days of soft fields painted with wildflowers and butterflies. Sierra Sommers will be so proud.

Dear God (again), Please tell Mother I am eternally unable to forgive.

Cindy - Here is where her essence abruptly ended. My thoughts crumble into dust and scatter among time and wreckage across the following blank pages in her diary. She was suddenly and totally gone. Her life in words vanished into oblivion. Her soul disappeared. Yet, decades after she wrote this, I can still feel her pain. The journey through the inner thoughts of my Mother evaporated into the stark emptiness of aging blank white pages in her diary. In my mind, it was as if she died once again.

Sophie left town early on June 26, 1962. Her car was found at the train station on the north side of DeLand.

Yet, within the diary, I saw life through her eyes and into her soul. Her story took me back in time to get to know and love her better than anyone. Her bravery and intellect now survive within me. I had nearly resigned to never finding her, and now I have renewed my goal to never give up on anything. My challenge is what to do with the story and how to live as and honor the Sierra Sommers in so many young and not-so-young women.

But then it also accompanies endless guilt for surviving and contributing to the death of a 16-year-old and ending the aspirations of the most important person in my life. Being attacked that evening of June 25th may have been her impetus for running away, but giving birth to me was a direct cause of her demise. As much as I wish to punish those who attacked her, my contribution of being born does not feel much better presently. Perhaps our simultaneous coexistence was not within the realm of nature, physics, or God.

After a long, deep breath, without conscious thought as to why, I loosened the brown paper covering the diary. There was yet more folded paper beneath it. I gently removed five aged documents my Mother had placed there decades ago. They contained information she wanted no one else to see – and I had my own "Eureka" moment! And then ... a small black and white photograph relented its long-held hiding spot, peeked out, and slid face up upon the table. It was a picture of Sophie kissing Winslow - another photo Jonathan had no doubt also taken on her 15th birthday.

I was thrilled, surprised, and wondering if she was symbolically kissing me for finding her life story...... ortelling me goodbye.

ANOTHER LIFE

Onism - Frustration of living in one body that inhabits only one place at a time.

I spent a quiet evening alone with the long-sought documents and reflected upon the written contents of the diary. I needed some time to recover emotionally before talking with Jonathan. My thoughts were with the courageous, imaginative trailblazer of my Mother, Sophie Sherman.

The next afternoon, I finally made a reluctant call to Jonathan (although he still fits the name of "Randy" or Randal) to request he stop by my home so I could show him what I found.

He arrived within thirty minutes. We sat at my dining room table after smiling, getting a hug, and playing with Lazlo.

"Jonathan, I finished reading the diary. The final entry is a long and challenging read. Remember the boys who "tossed her around"- it sounds as if they may have been much more aggressive than that. She was forcibly held down in a wooded area and gagged by who she vaguely describes as three older boys. After the boys left, she ran home barefoot.

Once home, Walters was remarkably less than concerned about her well-being. She does not provide lots of details, but he was physically abusive, grabbed her, and called her "less than polite" names. When

Winslow came to her defense, Walters kicked the puppy across the room, and she hit the piano. Sophie managed to get away from Walters, pick up the puppy, run upstairs, and lock herself in her room. Later, she buried Winslow under the Magnolia tree in her front yard that night.

Jonathan, if you wish to read it, you may. But I cannot recommend it."

"Cindy," he hung his head and said, "When she came over that night, I offered to wake my parents and take her to the hospital – but she was afraid Walters would get even more upset as he contributed to the abuse as well. And then, she would still have to leave anyway. It was a long time ago, and she was crying through some of this, but I do not recall her mentioning anything about rape – and I would remember that. Her clothes were clean and intact. Other than a two-inch cut on her arm, which was bruised and oozing a bit of blood, some scratches on her lower legs – which I attributed to her running through the woods - and being quite emotionally upset, there was little indication of serious physical harm."

"Everything she wrote supports that. The incident with the boys happened at about 7:30 p.m. that evening. Upon running home, and after the altercation with Walters, she took a shower and cleaned up before she came to your house about midnight – when Walters was passed out on the couch as usual," I said.

"And as if being confrontational with Sophie was not enough, Walters killed the dog. That bastard!" He paused and grabbed a Kleenex to blow his nose.

"I cannot imagine what may have happened to her if you had not been there to help. You saved her life, her life story, and gave her a way out," I gave him time to regain himself.

"She saw my light on and came over to talk. It was nearly midnight. She gave me her book – she read lots of books. We now know it was her diary for safekeeping – I placed it into the bottom of my footlocker that I was starting to pack. My parents drove me back to college early in the morning with that footlocker. My genuine concern was with her at that time. She also refused to let me call the police. She was terrified of Walters and his temper – and she had just experienced how much he could hurt her. (His eyes were closed as he relived and replayed the event in detail).

"She was upset and sobbing but determined to stay with relatives she knew not too far away. She said she would be safe there. That sounded like a great idea at the time. But she would not tell me where it was. She had her car and plenty of gas. I thought she would drive there – someplace not too far away. However, her car was later found at the train station.

She asked if I had a suitcase. I gave her one and twenty dollars. I had just sold a guitar and had more money than I needed. She requested I ask my parents to watch over her father – after all this, she was still worried about her slug of a father. And I understand why she did not mention the incident with her dog, but I wish she had. This whole thing was much more than a moderate squabble with her father and some boys teasing her. She left to return to her home about an hour after arriving.

"I told my parents about this incident when they woke early to take me back to school. We all went together early that morning to check on Sophie - sure enough, Walters was passed out on the couch, but Sophie and her Studebaker car were gone. And there was no sign of the dog, so I assumed she took Winslow with her. The police did show up to talk to Walters soon after that. My parents called them to report Sophie missing when they returned home." His eyes were closed.

Jonathan took a long, deep breath before continuing. "Cindy, I never heard from her again. I just thought she arrived safely at her family's home – but had no clue where that was. My parents moved away a few weeks later and had minimal contact with Walters. I do remember that he mumbled to them once that Sophie had gone away to school. We knew he had the financial means to do that. Sophie would have liked to do that. I was happy to hear it!"

I replied, "I likewise wish that had been true. Also, looking at the timing nine months later, it is not easy to accept that one of these testosterone tyrannical assholes (and not entirely excluding the possibility of dear old granddad) is possibly my father. However, after decades of searching for my father, I now accept that knowing may not be what I want."

Jonathan took a deep breath. "Cindy, I swear, I had no idea this event had anything to do with you being brought into this world. When she spoke with me, she was tearful but logical and had thought this out. She had a plan and her signature of ample determination. I had to agree that spending some time with almost anyone else and away from Walters wasn't a bad choice for her at that point. Walters could be unpleasant, but I did not realize how horrible. She did not deserve this. No one does. DeLand was a small town where family and neighbors solved such problems."

"Jonathan, please, I am so very grateful you were there. You rescued her. She admired you tremendously. You were her Prince Charming and inspiration, and hope to become more, do more, and learn more. While growing up, you listened to her; you were the one who asked what she thought, how things were going, and what her plans were. She wanted women to break into new careers everywhere because of you. She was at the library at Stetson earlier that day to see if she could find more information about Princeton University," I said.

"Princeton?" he asked.

"Princeton. She had been awarded a four-year scholarship there." I said.

He nodded with a hint of a sad smile.

"Sophie found five documents in the top drawer in Walters's bedroom when she went to remove the bullets and the handgun he kept there. There were also two sets of baby clothes and shoes, and cards from friends and more there," I told him.

"Wait. She took a gun to keep it away from Walters?"

"Yes, there was an incident of him shooting the mirrors in the house one night. The Police were unable to find the gun – or Sophie. She was hiding in her closet. But she knew where he kept the gun," I said. "This was in May 1962 – after Miss Ellie died. She planned to sell the gun and ammo at the pawn shop nearby. That way, they were no longer in the house, and she had some money to leave town."

Jonathan sat still with his mouth half open.

"OK – it gets much more interesting! So, stay tuned, as this becomes quite an amazing story," I said. "So, let's get on to some fascinating information showing how brave and remarkable Sophie was. She mentions in her diary about finding some documents. I found them hidden under the brown paper cover on the diary." I spread out the five documents on the table:

"And - Drum Roll, please!" I requested. Jonathan did a short drum roll on the tabletop.

#1. "Here is the very elusive, never seen before (or at least not recently), long-hidden original **Birth Certificate** for one **Saufi Irene Sherman**! She was born on March 9, 1947, along with her identical twin sister at DeLand Memorial Hospital. Her birth weight is two ounces less than that of her sister. But note the spelling of her first name. It is **Saufi, not Sophie.**

"The different spelling of Saufi explains the issues finding her birth certificate at County Records. These were not filed alphabetically by last name - but more like scattered and then heaped. As Sherman was a common name in this county, I was looking for "Sophie." Everyone thought she spelled her name as S-o-p-h-i-e – including Sophie herself. It is likely early on that Miss Ellie spelled it this way for her. I had tried every variation of the spelling I could think of – but as Camille was of French Cajun descent in Louisiana, perhaps she spelled it with a bit of French pronunciation." There is also mention of this being a twin birth – with a sister." Jonathan leaned in to look at the document.

#2. "There was one document folded very tightly and placed into the spine of the diary. It is the original **Birth Certificate** for **Sharline Ivy Sherman.** Sharline weighs two ounces more than her identical twin sister. Her twin sister is also mentioned in this document. Sharline has a small irregular birthmark on her upper right thigh. Notice it is spelled "Sharline".

Sophie mentions in her diary that she took extra precautions to hide this document well. She mentioned how she might burn it," I said.

"I also brought my photocopy of the torn and incomplete Sharline's Birth Certificate I obtained from the county office. The one provided in the diary is much more complete. The little info on the copy is included on the certificate Sophie provided."

"She tried to hide this certificate. Why would she do that." Jonathan flatly stated, without a question mark.

"To protect herself," I replied.

"From?" Jonathan was adding to the ongoing thought.

"Her entire world.... But stay tuned. More is coming up about that," I finished. He turned his head as a dog does to a strange sound.

"Then there was the day the Ambulance and Police came on February 23, 1951," I continued.

#3. "Here is the original **Police Report** of that day. The Police report includes Camille admitting to pushing Sharline "down into Hell" and pointing to the bottom of the basement stairs where the child was lying. "She had the mark of the devil."

#4. "Here is the original **Ambulance Report** of the same day. Ambulance notes state Camille is disoriented, irrational, and forcibly restrained to be taken for transfer and admission into a hospital in Chattahoochee, Florida.

These pages have been apparently torn from a three-ring binder – very likely the same one in the old records room of the Police Department I visited. Interestingly, no record existed there regarding any Police or Ambulance call that day to Sophie's home. My guess is Walters had connections to ensure the newspaper did not gain access to this information. "

Jonathan looked over the documents and shook his head. "Yes, I recall the day."

I continued, "OK, hang in there. I promise to make this interesting."

#5. "Here is the **Death Certificate of Sharline Ivy Sherman of February 23, 1951, the same day the Ambulance and Police arrived.**

Cause of death: *Posterior skull fracture.*

The Coroner Report states: "*Female child appears of stated age of three or four years. Evidence of posterior skull fracture occurred as the child hit concrete flooring following descent downstairs. Additionally, several body trauma marks are consistent with a recent fall down wooden stairs, a significant right ear infection, and apparent cigarette burns to three* *distal toe areas on the right foot. No other exterior areas or identifying marks are found on the body."*

"No wonder she cried a lot." Jonathan closed his eyes briefly and said, "Camille smoked cigarettes – I remember this now. She smoked incessantly. But why would she burn...." his voice faded to a stop. He closed his eyes.

"Those are the five documents Sophie found in Walters's drawer in his bedroom – along with his gun and ammo. But wait, there is more!" I said.

"Here is what I obtained from the Ocala hospital that Sophie was taken to in March 1963. Jonathan, you certainly may read this if you wish, but it may be best if I go through the highlights." He chose to read it silently to himself.

#6. Emergency Room Notes, Ocala, Florida - March 30, 1963 – A young adult female was found in a semi-conscious state at the bottom of stairs in a condemned building. She is lethargic and says, "Sharleen," and arrives via ambulance at the hospital with an elevated temperature. She is found to be post-partum and possibly septic with a severe head injury post-fall. Her driver's license, in her pocket, indicates her name is Sophie Sherman. She does respond when called "Sophie." A small mirror is also in her pocket, which likely broke during her fall.

When asked about a baby, she nods yes. Police are sent to the scene to search for an infant. The infant was found upstairs in the same building and brought to the Emergency Room with a tattered rag doll and a small towel with SM or WS (depending on which it faced) hand embroidered on it. The female infant appears about two weeks old and healthy. A shoestring is tied on what is left of the umbilical cord. A Nurse placed the baby beside her Mother about 45 minutes before Sophie succumbed to her injuries.

Before her death, Sophie mentions a possible husband named Randal Peterson. This person is not found locally. Information from her driver's license is used to locate Sophie's father, Walters Sherman, in DeLand. He admits to Sophie being his daughter but refuses to consent to treatment. He does not acknowledge her current age (16 is indicated on the driver's license) or any past medical history regarding her. He would not provide information regarding anyone named Randal Peterson or Sharleen and declined to accept care of the infant. He was informed of the critical condition of Sophie and reported for next-of-kin purposes; a death certificate for Sophie and a birth certificate for the baby will likely be sent to him via mail. He provided his attorney's name and phone number and hung up the telephone.

For temporary identification purposes, the infant is named Cindy (by nursing staff after "Cinderella") Peterson (anticipating the location of the Father). No Randy or Randal Peterson of 18 to 35 years of age is readily found in Ocala, Florida – other than one currently enlisted in Military Service and has been out of the country for the past two years.

Shortly after that, Sophie became unresponsive, experienced a grand mal seizure, and passed away.

We took a break for a few minutes as Jonathan processed this information, asked questions, and regained his composure.

#7. "A copy of the **Death Certificate of Sophie Sherman Peterson of March 30, 1963,** that I obtained from county records in Ocala, Florida for Sophie Sherman (Peterson)," I said.

I looked at Jonathan and said, "Please, this is disturbing, so I will point out just the important parts if you wish." Being the professional he is, he quickly read the following documents:

Cause of death: Severe frontal skull fracture post-fall down a flight of stairs.

The Coroner Report states: *"This female appears of the listed age of 16 years. Injury of bruising and abrasions consistent with unwitnessed apparent fall on wooden stairs and with concrete landing within a condemned building. The evident head injury is consistent with x-ray findings of frontal skull fracture and local hemorrhage. Medics at the scene stated the stairs were in poor repair. There is no indication of violence. An incidental finding of a small, irregular birthmark is found on the anterior upper right thigh, not* *associated with trauma. The patient is post-partum for approximately two weeks.*

#8. Birth Certificate for Cindy Peterson

Date of birth – Unknown, approximately March 14, 1963. **Location Unknown:** probably Florida. **Birth Weight:** Unknown. **APGAR Score:** Unknown. Birth unattended. **Female.** Healthy. Mother is likely Sophie Sherman Peterson. "Nothing further is completed on the form," I said.

"Jonathan, remember you said you never discussed her twin sister with her? You were unsure if she knew or remembered that she had a sister. She knew it and so much more."

Jonathan replied, "There were upsetting things we did not want her to know that we knew. But then – she also was so very, very smart."

"Allow me to show you something she didn't tell you or anyone - and just how very astute she was. Stay with me on this," I said.

I put both Saufi/Sophie and Sharline's birth certificates and death certificates closer before us.

"See on the documents where Sharline had a birthmark at birth, but there is no mention of it on her Death Certificate or Coroner Report?" I said.

"That could just be an innocent oversight," said Jonathan. "It happens."

"Sophie had no indication of a birthmark when she was born. But there is mention of one in the same location and description as Sharline's at birth on Sophie's Coroner Report," I pointed out.

He re-checked the documents and looked a bit both bewildered and surprised—two different Coroners at different places and different times.

"Please allow me to provide more insight," I said. I had Sophie's diary nearby with key entries marked with a small piece of paper. "Here are some diary entries that may help further," I said.

I read out loud to Jonathan:

May 15, 1962: I remember the day. Mrs. Williston from next door came to see how she could help with the commotion. I remember sitting on the kitchen floor, holding my Sophie doll, and crying for my hurt sister. Mrs. Williston picked me up and took me away from the scene of my crumpled sister below on the basement floor. She held me and asked the name of the doll I was holding tightly. "Sophie," I said. Mrs. Williston has called me Sophie ever since. My sister held her Sharline doll and lay motionless at the bottom of the stairs. In the background, my mother was screaming about pushing my sister down the stairs because she had "the mark of the devil" over and over, and soon, the Ambulance came.

About that time, a Policeman came into the room with Mrs. Williston and me. He asked her questions and the child's name at the bottom of the stairs. I was afraid and started crying. Where was he taking my sister? Was he going to take me away, too? Mrs. Williston told the Police Officer that Sharline was at the bottom of the steps and my name was Sophie. Even then, I wondered if it was intentional in case Mother found out.

And posted in the diary later that same day...

Memories flood my brain. We had matching cloth dolls with brown yarn hair, blue dresses, and matching bloomers – but we could tell them apart because one had a spot on her leg. Once we were separated from sharing one large crib to sleeping in matching separate beds in the same room, we kept each other's doll to feel like we were still together. We were about three years old then. Back before words were needed, we shared silently between our intertwined souls.

Then, there is her very final entry on June 25, 1962.

Dear God (again), please tell Mother I am eternally unable to forgive.

Jonathan examines Sharline's Birth and Sophie's Death Certificates carefully again. He placed them in his lap, closed his eyes, and leaned back. "An irrational belief versus a meaningless birthmark. Sophie was not Sophie at all. **She was one courageous kid who outsmarted all of us to protect herself and her sister."**

"Let me read to you what else she wrote in her diary," I said as I opened another bookmarked page – also on May 15, 1962...

"One time, Miss Ellie told me that the truth may set you free, but it seldom makes you happy. My mother intended to kill me, and father treated me as an annoyance. What would have happened without Miss Ellie?...

I said, "Apparently, Walters did not interact with his children enough to tell them apart on the day the ambulance came. So, they all took a one-word response from a not quite 4-year-old as reality without question. She became and grew up as her sister. She likely learned how to say Sophie before her own actual name. Sophie was the most important person in her life. Walters believed she was Sophie. There is nothing to indicate otherwise," I continued.

"Everyone believed she was Sophie," Jonathan quietly replied.

"So, Sharline with the "mark of the devil" grew up as Sophie. I wonder how Camille would feel about being so outwitted by a young child. And to keep from being alone in a lonely world, she became her sister. So, it makes sense how the Birth and Death Certificates of Sharline and the birthmark situation threatened her identity. That is why she took extra precautions to hide it and considered burning it." Jonathan was putting the carefully placed pieces of her bifurcated life together.

I added, "And why she gave you her diary with the documents under the cover to protect it after she left home and escaped from Walters and ventured into the unknown."

Jonathan went on, "I assumed her life was nearly typical – being a very bright only child... albeit of local stature and influence of a father prone to occasional drunken bouts and a doting Nanny. Without local relatives and in a large home, I thought while perhaps lonely, her needs were met on a physical level anyway, and she had well-defined interests and ambitions for her life.... up until the evening she was attacked."

I added, "She ticked off all the right boxes. She was a bright young lady. She had the prominence, placement, presentation, and proximity to maintain a community-wide deception and to prevent her father from ever realizing the truth. There was no reason not to believe her; those near her loved her enough to accept and never question such things. And while her identity would never change my thoughts of her, I am frightened to think about what Walters would have done if he discovered that "Sophie was not Sophie.""

"Cindy," Jonathan said, "have you considered that she was in Ocala because she was trying to get back home from wherever she had been." It was more of a statement than a question.

There were a few moments of silence between us. "That is a profound possibility," I said, in half a trance.

"I admit, I wondered if she did not return home in an attempt to protect me (and herself) from Walters.

Also, a small, cracked mirror was found in her pocket in the Emergency Room after she fell down the stairs."

"Oh – KAY? Jonathan asked. "Sophie was a beautiful young lady, but not someone who impressed me as being obsessed with her appearance."

"There were no pictures of her sister - individually or the two of them together. She talked with her sister often in the vanity mirror in her bedroom in Walters's home." And then my words caught up with the thought. "She brought her sister with her within that mirror!" I said.

"I wish I had paid better attention to Sophie at the time. I wish I had been wiser then." Jonathan was verbally beating himself.

"Jonathan, she would not tell Miss Ellie that she was Sharline. She was afraid of Walters – and rightfully so. She had things under control until the day the "boys" attacked her, and then Walters joined in with more abuse. And you were the only person on the planet who did help her that day. Sophie decided to leave. I cannot say that I would not have done the same." I replied.

"Why did no one ever contact my family about Sophie?" Jonathan said.

"You said it yourself – there were few well-organized social services then. And it was easy to believe she left for a private school. Walters was a Class A Jerk and lived alone for nine more miserable years before he died. She would have been 25 years old by that time. He never told anyone she had died, other than his attorney and estate manager, and it was easy to believe she had moved on with her life elsewhere." I said.

"During that time, Walters never attempted to contact me – or, apparently, attempted to find Sophie. So, imagine my surprise when an attorney came out of nowhere to tell me one day about inheriting his estate." I replied.

"Jonathan, I also see this as Sophie's innovatively brilliant creation for twin girls to grow up together. They protected each other and talked with each other in the mirror and in the water at what is now Blue Spring Park. She often referred to herself as "we," and a Medium in Cassadaga, and her school friend who accompanied her on that visit asked Sophie about her sister. So, while you were safeguarding the past from her, she was keeping her present from you. The Medium did tell Sophie that "Jonathan will be the messenger. Go to him," during that visit in May of 1962. Sophie had no idea that "Jonathan" was you - aka Randal - but nonetheless, yes, you were the messenger she brought her diary to," I said.

Eventually, a hint of a smile found his face. "I believe I warned you to be prepared to be surprised when you read her diary."

"This has truly been the most amazing journey of my life. And I owe every bit of it to you. Thank you, Jonathan, for bringing her to life for me."

On a personal level, I became painfully aware that despite her story and experience, once again, all the generations of my entire family came down to one person. Me.

Later, more occurred to me regarding who my Mother, Sophie, truly was. She was living with a name given to her by someone other than her mother. The neighbor at home the day the ambulance and police came called her Sophie. Both the birth and death certificates verify that my Mother may have lived as Sophie, but she was born Sharline. Perhaps she perpetuated this to appease others and to protect herself. Who can blame her? Sophie refused to wear clothing that might expose her birthmark.

How could she not remember her identical twin sister? They shared the same large crib and later slept in similar twin beds in her bedroom. Later, the two girls in the mirror giggled and shared secrets. They shared more than heritage. They each suffered for the other. They had joined souls yet were physically separate and out of step in time. Each was deprived of the other. And each died of tragically similar injuries.

I recall researching newspapers and public records. I had found some scant mention of a "Sharlene" Sherman in Arizona that coincided with when Sophie was missing from home. At the time, I disregarded it as another person – thinking Arizona was too far away. But then, even her final Ocala hospital records originally had "Sharleen" with a line through it and "Sophie" handwritten above it. When the ambulance personnel came for her at the bottom of the apartment stairs in Ocala, Florida, she mumbled, "Sharleen." Perhaps the wrong name (and spelling of it) was attributed to her head injury. Maybe she was throwing Walters off her trail and simultaneously openly mocking him.

The journey through the inner thoughts of my Mother abruptly evaporated into stark nothing on Monday, June 25, 1962. Yet, despite its brevity, secrets, and challenges, Sophie's life was a remarkable one of colossal courage, hope, and grace among immense social change and family unrest. It was also an arduous journey that found a way into the present - and within me. My challenge is encouraging the Sierra Sommers in many young girls and women today.

How many people experience their mother's joys, pains, experiences, feelings, and tribulations while she was growing up? I no longer feel deprived of a Mother. I now know and love Mother deeper than anyone ever could. I am no longer a lost orphan but rather a crusader through time! And I can hear Sierra saying, "Make the journey as important as the destination."

FAVORITE ANGELS

Yesterday, I sat at home alone and quietly reviewed Sophie's story and how she mastered a triple role of complementary lives. She was herself, her sister, and the full-time manager to maintain the illusion while living two lives simultaneously.

The door opened shortly after a soft knock, and Jonathan entered. "Cindy, I just came by to check on you and see how things were going," he said.

I sighed. "I never thought finding the truth about my Mother could make me feel so sad, angry, lonely, and proud at once," I responded. "I wonder if she was terrified to tell anyone the truth, thinking perhaps Walters would kill her. How awful is it to live life as someone else – while realizing you were the one who was intended to die?"

"Or perhaps it was an honorable way to keep her sister alive to others and herself despite it all." Jonathan was always more philosophical.

"She said something interesting that night she came to see me before she left town. Miss Ellie once told her that Hell is where God trains his very best Angels. She qualifies as an Angel doing that training. Cindy, your Mother, was a remarkable young lady who found a way to bring you into the world. There is so much of her alive in you. The caring for others, the smarts, wit, and boundless determination. Look in the mirror, Cindy. She is with you."

"She also said the best people return as the happiest and most beloved puppies," I responded.

"Allow me to attempt to summarize," I continued quickly. "Her mother, Camille, kills her sister. Her father brutally berates and beats her after a horrific ordeal with a gang of frisky young guys. Winslow, the puppy, meets with a violent death in her defense. And the probable name of my biological dad remains within a tribe of anonymous hooligans.

"However, she left me with a fabulous story where a young lady gave up on becoming a Princess in a castle and managed to escape death, violence, insanity, gang rape, abuse, and murder, and took on and outwitted a heartless world by herself - with help from Miss Ellie.

"Previously, and despite understanding my intended name is likely Winslow Sherman, I had been reluctant to change it to one associated with madness, mayhem, and murder. Now, I see the greater courage, stamina, wisdom, and determination of what a young woman endured to protect her sister. So, yesterday, I submitted the paperwork to change my name from Cindy Peterson to Winslow Sherman," I paused. "I try to downplay the part about being named after a dog – but she was no ordinary puppy!"

"My Mother and I have a twisted legacy of incorrect names. She changed her name from Sharline to

Sophie. I am changing mine from what hospital Nurses named me to what my Mother intended. And I owe unraveling a decades-long mystery all to you with my very sincerest gratitude.

"Thank you, Jonathan. You provided the meaning to make my life whole. I am well beyond humbled. My sense of abandonment has transformed into an endless love for and from a Mother I never knew in person and within a delightful city that celebrates its past. I have spent decades searching for her, and you found her for me," I said.

"May I interest you in a celebratory trip to Rodeo Whip for some Rocky Road ice cream?" I asked.

He provided a gentle smile in affirmation. "I love Rocky Road ice cream – and accept any excuse to get some!"

BENEATH THE MAGNOLIA

A few days later, I felt compelled to visit the home that Sophie had shared with her father. From the sidewalk, it is a two-story vintage home that was no doubt more than charming and, in the present day, an accepted reminder of a grander era in DeLand. I wondered what unwritten stories, times, and tales took place there. Then I noticed a mirror I could see through a second-story window reflecting the large Magnolia tree in the front yard. It was no doubt the present-day Magnolia sapling that Sophie and Miss Ellie had planted so long ago. I may have some roots here after all. Sophie was right to plant something to outlive herself.

At the risk of invading the present-day homeowners' area, I hugged the tree trunk, sat on the slightly damp ground beneath ample foliage, and quietly wept. In short order, a mature lady rushed outside from the home's front door and inquired what was wrong – and what she could do. There were no words to explain except for me to say, "Once upon a time, my Mother lived here."

The kind lady introduced herself as Laura Langston and explained that she and her late husband bought the house from a prominent older man who had died in 1972.

"He was my grandfather, Walters Sherman." I tried to regain my composure and said, "My Mother, Sophie

Sharline Sherman (I decided just at that moment to call her by both names to credit each), lived here with him. She planted this tree in 1956.

Laura was quiet momentarily and responded, "We found a sealed glass jar buried beneath this tree with a note in it. I brought it into the house years ago to keep the elements from destroying the note. Do you know who Winslow is? Wait! Let me get it. I remember right where it is – just a moment. Please don't go anywhere!"

She returned with an old glass Green's Dairy milk bottle with a metal, somewhat rusty cap tied to the top. She said that the inside of the bottle had been stuffed with scraps from a poodle skirt at one point. She presented a yellowed, one-page, tattered note written in familiar handwriting. It read –

To Winslow – I shall always love you more than life itself and across all time and distance. You make the world a better place. Love is the only thing that lives in the past and present and continues unchanged throughout all eternity. I share with you all my hopes and dreams until we meet again. SS.

I leaned back on my hands in the dirt, looked up to the sky through magnolia "angel tree" leaves, fighting off tears, and took a long, deep breath as a flock of birds soared before a soft pastel rainbow.

"I am her daughter, Winslow," I said. This further proves that God's Motherless children have a bond that extends beyond this life and world.

"Then I am happy to be the very late messenger to finally deliver the note to the proper person!" she replied.

After a lifetime of searching for my long-deceased Mother, she ultimately finds me again with an eternal bond that echoes beyond time.

It wasn't until then that my tears permitted me to take note of Laura's colorful costume apparel. She noticed my expression – and responded before my inquiry.

"Oh! I work with the children's theater in Athens Theater. We are doing a play about dreams coming true – and they needed a Fairy Godmother. Voila!" She swooped her arms down her full sequined dress and shook her glittered hair.

A vortex engulfed my consciousness and entire being as I became completely speechless. Disney has nothing to compete with half a century of lost reality coming together and returning home for the first time.

Laura had to rush off to the play and invited me to stay under the tree as long as needed and take the note and milk bottle with me. She also asked if she could call me later. I agreed and gave her my cell phone number.

So, this is how it feels to be the last branch of my Sherman family tree. The one remaining blossom (myself) is sitting in the dirt under the tree planted decades ago by my Mother. I am home. And it is much more beautiful than any castle ever imagined.

I confirmed so many years after her death that Sophie lived the life of another for most of her 16 years. While growing up, I often dreamed of my Mother and imagined she was reaching out to me.

With the salvation of Miss Ellie, my Mother endured murder, violence, mental illness, and a heartless life at home – and yet learned and lived gentle compassion. Within Sierra Sommers, she created adventure, altruism, and an escape to a world she crafted to share with others. From Randal (alias Jonathan), she gained respect for life, career, and ambition. I owe my life to them. Every person plays a role in creating the future – even those who dig up and save an old milk bottle with a note in it.

A few days later, Laura did call and requested we talk. One of the reasons she and her husband bought this house, formerly belonging to my grandfather Walters, is because her aunt, Mrs. Williston, used to live next door. Her Aunt had told Laura and Laura's mother that she was convinced Walters Sherman had killed Sophie. He was violent and nasty, and – POOF – one day Sophie was gone (even when out of costume, her Fairy Godmother persona magnified an almost magical "poof" over the phone.)

"I would be most grateful for any information you could share!" I replied.

We met at her home the next day. I felt I knew the place well as I walked through the doorway. I could see the mantel on which the "now" clock ticked, the area where the couch that Walter slept upon no doubt was, the back-porch area of the "fairy tale" lunch for Miss Ellie's birthday lunch, and the location of the garden in the back yard that Sophie attended, and Winslow, the dog, scattered piles of fallen leaves.

The contents of her time had been replaced with more modern microwaves, computers, sectional furniture, and more – but as the scented breeze came through large wood-framed open windows, the floors creaked, and the feeling of Sophie's time and her essence were still very present. I tried to imagine Sophie slowly walking down the elegant stairwell, dressed to go to the high school prom she had never attended.

We sat at a vintage Victorian dining table with elegantly carved chairs beneath a large bronze and crystal chandelier. Laura started with, "My Auntie so loved Sophie. My Auntie was the neighbor who came to her home the day the ambulance and police took Camille Sherman and her twin sister away. Auntie told me all about that day. She knew the twins' names, but they were still so young that she could not tell them apart.

"Seeing the police, ambulance crew, and the motionless child at the bottom of the stairs, she picked up the sobbing, uninjured twin sitting on the kitchen floor at the top of the basement stairs. (Laura pointed to the spot.) Auntie carried her into another room – right over there to that Study room (she pointed to her right), so the poor child would not see the horrific scene of her sister at the bottom of the stairs. At the same time, Mrs. Sherman, Camille, was screaming about the child at the bottom of the stairs being possessed or something that made no sense. Two policemen were trying to calm Camille down."

Tears were filling my eyes as I saw the actual set and knew the well-narrated scene so well.

"Once in a quieter area and away from the ruckus, my Auntie gently sat down with the child in her arms and asked her, "What is the name of the pretty doll you are holding?"

She said, "Sophie" – which is how Auntie knew it was Sharline who died."

I stopped myself from commenting. Miss Ellie had said that belief often won over truth. I believed my silence was what my Mother would want.

This also verified what Sophie had written of that day in her diary. The diary confirmed it was here that Mrs. Williston unwittingly furthered the misidentify. First, Camille was irrational and confused as to which child was which. Walters was likely not involved enough to help. Perhaps the surviving Sharline accepted the name of her deceased sister, Saufi (albeit with a different spelling), out of fear. And her verbal skills at the time did not include the vocabulary to correct the situation. The misidentification on the death certificate of the child at the bottom of the stairs further sealed the fate of the actual Sophie. It was beyond the control or influence of a child of such a young age. She lived the life of another to protect her sister - and herself.

Laura asked what I knew of my grandfather, Walters. I responded I had never met him, but I knew he was not the most pleasant or sociable in his "golden" years.

Laura continued. "Walters did become increasingly belligerent as the years passed. He would throw things in the house and yell at no one. My Auntie told me that one day Walters pooped on her prized petunias in her front yard. He would run through the yard naked and pass out on the front lawn. He burned things from the house in a large blaze in the backyard several months after Sophie disappeared. He scared people. We were all happy when his car finally broke down, and he stopped driving on the sidewalks and through fences. I firmly believe that if you allow some people to have their way long enough, they will self-destruct. I suppose it is possible that misery was his only comfort. I cannot imagine what Sophie must have endured living with that man," she said quietly and politely, pausing to allow me to process this.

I sighed and said, "Apparently, Sophie told Walters about some boys "teasing" her. But being a less-than-pleasant soul sometimes, Walters beat her. So, she drove her car away early the next morning. Never to be seen here again." I tried to explain concisely.

"She also did write in her diary about walking Mrs. Williston to church and how very, very kind your Aunt was to her. Thank you so much on her behalf for that," I replied.

It was Laura's turn to sigh. "I wish Sophie had spoken with my Auntie; I am sure Sophie could have stayed with her. (I silently nodded in agreement.) I heard that Sophie's car was found at the railroad station – but Sophie was gone and never found and never returned home. It was also about when the Petersons on the other side of her home moved away. Randal Peterson was a nice young man, but several years older, who looked over Sophie too."

Laura continued, "After Sophie disappeared, Walters became less able to care for himself. His house was a mess. He was a bigger mess and barely coherent at times. He was angry and belligerent and anything but charitable or considerate of others. He would yell at my Auntie and call her names. She sprayed him with a hose to get him away from her house. But she was also not without some compassion. In the late afternoon, she would sneak in the back door of this home (back when he was living here) to leave a pan of food for him in the kitchen –

which he would eat. During the same trip, she would also retrieve her usually empty pan of food she had left for him the previous day.

"My mother and I visited Auntie the afternoon Walters was found dead in his home in 1972. I was about 16 years old at the time, and I was not convinced Auntie had not played a role in Walters's death. She had left a homemade casserole for him the day before he died. She returned to his home the next morning to retrieve her nearly empty casserole pan - but apparently without a replacement next meal. She found him lifeless on the floor. She brought the pan of mostly eaten casserole home and called the police.

"When my mother and I visited her that day, what was left of the casserole my Auntie had made for him was soaking in her kitchen sink. An empty bottle of sleeping pills was on the kitchen counter nearby. My mother had brought the medication to my Auntie from the pharmacy two days before. She asked Auntie about the drug. My Auntie said she had spilled the entire contents of the bottle on the floor and thrown all the pills away. The three of us exchanged glances, and from that day forward, we agreed to an unspoken secret about what may have happened to those pills.

"My Auntie died in her house several years after Walters died here. She was almost 86 years old," she said. "Some very kind people bought Auntie's home soon after and still live there today. But we did get to live next to Auntie and help and enjoy her during her last few years. And my husband and I loved this house! But unfortunately, he passed away two years ago."

"When we bought this house, it had been empty for a while and was all cleaned out," she said. "The only thing we found was the jar with the note in the front yard in the dirt beneath the Magnolia.

"The entire town was looking for Sophie, missing her, and wondering what happened. The rumors were that either she went out of town to a private school or Walters had killed her. She did not come back when Walters died. Do you know what became of her? If I may ask," Laura slowly asked.

I thought for a moment about how to best answer it. "She told a friend she was leaving town to stay with some relatives. And she had plans to use her scholarship to attend college. But while out of town, she fell down some stairs and hit her head. She died very shortly after that." Presently, it was all I cared to share with the world for now, and it generated a short but accepting response from Laura, who first gasped and said, "Just like her sister."

HOMEWARD BOUND

In Sherman Park, children play, and the community building provides crafts, education, and coupons to the nearby residents. Local artists were commissioned to create a sculpture area of children playing of various cultures being loved and enjoyed. There are swing sets, a sandbox, monkey bars, paved paths for tricycles, another for jogging and bicycles, hopscotch, a giant playhouse, exercise stations, an oversized tic-tac-toe board, and a gentle winding paved walking path throughout the trees. Today, that path accommodates a mother pushing her infant in a stroller and a young man strolling behind an elderly lady in a wheelchair.

The park feels as if it transforms time and space into an essence specific to the individual. I think of it as a gift from my Mother and grandfather that successfully conquers stress and provides happiness and comfort to make many people happy. I paid to have the park created with part of my inheritance from Walters Sherman – alias the grandfather I never met.

Recently, I recommissioned local artists to create some additional durable outdoor sculptures of the special relationship between young twin sisters having fun. There are new sculptures of two girls blowing dandelions, gathering wildflowers, sitting on a bench giggling, and playing with dolls under a tree. The Sister's Garden is near the picnic area and closest to our favorite picnic table under a massive Oak. It is where Antonio and I routinely meet each week in the afternoon to slow down, relax, listen to birds and the laughter of children, and catch up with life.

I recently requested the City Council's permission to rename the Park from Sherman Park to Sophie's Wildflowers. I also commissioned the artists to create sculptures of a wildflower garden, a child running with a toy plane, another with a toy sailboat named *Finding Hope*, yet another trying to fly a handmade kite of part palm frond, a few plastic straws precariously held together with drops of super glue, the small hole-less part of an old sheet, and a few rubber bands tied together for a tail. Also, soon, there will be sculptures of two dogs (one resembling Max, the other Winslow) sitting by a ball.

Today, Jonathan joined Antonio and me at our usual "catch up on life" lunch at our usual picnic table in the park.

I brought the routine local cuisine – Taco Bell. I also got more than the usual amount to have plenty for Jonathan. Soon after, Antonio showed up with two strawberry smoothies (one with extra whipped cream) and a large Coke for his Uncle Jonathan. After smiles and a hug, we relaxed in the breeze at the table, watched kids play on the playground, and admired the latest sculptures beneath trees. We talked about his clinic, how things were going, and various new ways he had found to help those in need. I thanked Antonio again for his role in helping me to find my Mother – and told him how I have proof that my Mother babysat for him!

Within moments, Jonathan joined us. He brought with him a cardboard box topped with a red bow. We did a group hug; Antonio gently patted his uncle's back. Jonathan was still smiling (a slightly crooked smile) when he placed the box on the picnic table as he sat down. I set out the food and drinks and took a moment to take in my adopted kinfolk's sights, sounds, and presence. I was simultaneously humbled and grateful to be considered family. We chatted and shared the latest events in our lives. Then, a smiling Jonathan changed the banter and spoke up.

"It is great to see my two favorite people again, and I have a bit of an announcement." He stood to say, "Ole Miss Johnson is a previous client of mine. She loved Boxer dogs, but they were too big to manage anymore. So, she got this (nodding to the box) three days before she fell and broke her hip."

"Miss Johnson is doing just fine but asked me to find the contents of this box a good home," he said between sips of Coke. Then, he looked at me and said, "I cannot think of anyone who can take better care of this little rascal than you. Besides, it is a bit of a birthday tradition for me." As on cue, a tiny white paw poked its way through the loose corner of the wiggling box.

"She is about four months old and needs a great best friend, and in a further twist of the mystery of life,

Miss Johnson had the fortuitous foresight to name her Sharline. She says you can spell that any way you like. And the dog takes her well-loved ragdoll with her everywhere."

Jonathan gently picked up the gyrating box and handed it to me as he and Antonio stood and sang Happy Birthday.

As I opened the box, a small white puppy jumped into my arms as happy excitement welcomed me with incessant motion and endless joy. She licked away my tears and put a grin on my face. Her wagging tail was everywhere at once. Happiness is no longer around the next corner. It is here. It is within me. It is my NOW.

After a long journey to find my roots, "home and family" found me. As of last week, documents state my official name is now Winslow Sherman. My home is not a magical castle in the clouds but rather a profound joy and contentment within me. I am convinced my

Mother's spirit resides within a happy puppy named Sharline.

Sharline and Winslow Sherman - together, at last.
https://pxhere.com/en/photo/956644

As this journey neared its happy ending, I wondered what words my Mother and Sierra would want to offer. I thought this may be appropriate:

"To every young lady, regardless of age, anxious to take on the world ahead and to the wisdom and the love of the Ms. Ellie's who encourage them to do so. Not the end – ever, but a new beginning – always. The adventure continues."

Sophie and Sharline Sherman & Sierra Sommers

Some favorite thoughts in words (Found in the back of the diary)

- *Wisdom is found in those rare times when it is OK to break the rules.*
- *There is much more to see without your eyes.*
- *Belief is powerful and can sway more minds than proof.*
- *Truth and happiness are not always best friends.*
- *God trains the best Angels within the depths of Hell.*
- *Love is intolerant of intolerance.*
- *Wisdom and kindness live in quiet places.*
- *The very best people come back as the happiest, most beloved puppies.*

AFTER WORD

No mention of Miss Ellie's last name is found. A search of the Internet, documents, burial sites, neighbors, and more provided no documentation of her. It appears her life evaporated from all records of the time except within this diary. Regardless, I am immensely grateful for her kind, gentle attention, and wise guidance of my Mother.

Look for Sharline and me in the **Annual DeLand Mardi Gras Dog Parade!**

To the adventures ahead!

Winslow Sherman (previously Cindy Peterson)

The Annual DeLand Dog Parade

WEST VOLUSIA HISTORICAL SOCIETY

THE
ATHENS THEATRE
1922

THIS HISTORICALLY SIGNIFICANT LANDMARK
OPENED IN 1922 AS A SILENT FILM/VAUDEVILLE
THEATRE. ONCE THE ENTERTAINMENT
CENTERPIECE OF THE COUNTY, THE ATHENS
OPERATED CONTINUOUSLY FOR NEARLY
SEVENTY YEARS, CHANGING ITS PROGRAMMING
OVER TIME AS TECHNOLOGY ADVANCED.
THE THEATRE WAS DEVELOPED BY L.M.
PATTERSON, A NATIVE OF WASHINGTON,
D.C., WHO MOVED TO DELAND IN 1920 AND
ORGANIZED THE DELAND MOVING PICTURE
COMPANY. DESIGNED BY MURRAY S. KING, A
PROMINENT ORLANDO ARCHITECT, THE
THEATRE WAS COMPLETED IN 1921. MUSIC
AND SOUND EFFECTS WERE PERFORMED ON
A LARGE WURLITZER ORGAN. THE OPENING
NIGHT PERFORMANCE ON JANUARY 6, 1922
FEATURED THE 7-REEL SILENT FILM, "THE
BLACK PANTHER'S CUB," A 4-ACT COMIC
PLAY, AND FOUR VAUDEVILLE ACTS.

DeLand -
Florida's First
Monarch City USA

STETSON UNIVERSITY
DELAND HALL
BUILT 1884
THE OLDEST BUILDING IN FLORIDA IN
CONTINUOUS USE FOR HIGHER EDUCATION
AND THE FIRST BUILDING ON THE STETSON
UNIVERSITY CAMPUS. ORIGINALLY HOUSED
THE LIBRARY, CHAPEL, CLASSROOMS, GYMNASIUM
AND OFFICES. LATER USED AS A WOMEN'S
RESIDENCE, KINDERGARTEN, SCHOOL OF MUSIC
AND THE ADMINISTRATIVE CENTER OF CAMPUS.
LISTED ON THE NATIONAL REGISTER OF
HISTORIC PLACES IN 1983.

NAVY F-14 TOMCAT

DELAND
NAVAL AIR
STATION
MUSEUM

VOLUSIA COUNTY

NAVY "DIVE BOMBER" PILOTS
WHO TRAINED IN VOLUSIA COUNTY
WERE PART OF EFFORTS ON TWO FRONTS
TO BRING WW II TO A CLOSE IN 1945.

AT ANY GIVEN TIME FROM 1942 - 1946,
NEARLY 3,000 OFFICERS AND ENLISTED MEN
TRAINED AT THE DeLAND AND DAYTONA BEACH NAVAL AIR STATIONS.
TWICE THAT MANY WOMEN WERE TRAINED
IN THE SECOND WOMEN'S ARMY AUXILIARY CORPS (WAAC)
IN DAYTONA BEACH FROM 1942 - 1943.

MEANWHILE, DAYTONA BEACH BOAT WORKS
HELPED WAR EFFORTS BY CONSTRUCTING SUBMARINE CHASERS
AND PATROL BOATS FOR THE NAVY.

THE LAST EXISTING SUBMARINE OBSERVATION TOWER
ON THE FLORIDA COAST STANDS IN ORMOND BEACH.

DeLand, Florida - Yesterday & Today

DeLand is a quaint college town that lives within its history. Its residents protect and cherish its past and natural resources as it lives gently in the present and into the future. Go to Google to search:

City of DeLand

Visit West Volusia

Things to do in DeLand

History of DeLand

DeLand Historic Mural Walk

West Volusia Historical Society

Florida Historical Society

Blue Spring State Park

DeLand Memorial Hospital & Veterans Museum

DeLand Naval Air Station Museum

DeLand Register of Historic Places

Gillespie Museum

Mardi Gras Dog Parade

Marineland

Monkey Island Sandford

Rodeo Whip Ice Cream

Southern Cassadaga Spiritualist Camp

Stetson Mansion

Stetson University

The Athens Theater

Tom's Pizza

Volusia County Fair

Woolworth's DeLand

Zoo, Sanford, Florida

About the Author:

Sahara Sutter is a university professor with a doctorate in health science. She admires the remarkable journeys through the everyday life of the unsung heroes who change the world for others daily. Perhaps childhood fairytales are stories of spiritual beings and human form, after all.

She supports the optimism of human ingenuity that strives to redefine and improve the future for all and make today's social accomplishments a reality.

Sophie's Wildflowers serves as a spiritual successor to her previous volume, Beyond the Garden - God's Houseplants.

Author's contact:
sahara@saharasutter.com

PHOTOGRAPHS AND CREDITS

Some photographs within this work came from various historical media for and regarding Florida. All photographs are within the Public Domain. Changes (with permission for specific photos) may have been made to size, crop, and color (black and white). Uncited photographs were taken and provided by Barbara Duffy with permission.

floridamemory.com

https://www.floridamemory.com/discover/photographs

The picture of a girl in a poodle skirt is Wikimedia commons:

https://commons.wikimedia.org/w/index.php?search=girl+wearing+poodle+skirt&title=Special:MediaSearch&go=Go&type=image

Photo is under a CC BY-SA 2.0 license. Credit: Tom Roy Hobbs from Field Of Dreams, USA.

Creative Commons Attribution-Share Alike 2.0

https://pixabay.com/photos/kiss-kisses-puppy-dog-young-lady-2685779/

Image by JackieLou DL from Pixabay

https://pixabay.com/photos/puppy-young-lady-kiss-kisses-2681767/

Image by JackieLou DL from Pixabay